STORIES HEARD IN THE ESTATE
A COLLECTION OF SHORT-STORIES

Dedicated to my beloved son,

Muhammad Idris Abdul-Ahad.

Whilst you dwell in the gardens playing with your cousin Ilyas, I am left saddened wondering about all of the adventures we were to have. I once imagined you would have been sat by the bookshelf in the front room of the house, with hair like your mothers, flicking through all of daddy's books. I know and believe with all of my heart that one day when I see you in the after-life you will take me and mummy on your adventures in Paradise.

We miss and love you dearly.

01/07/2021.

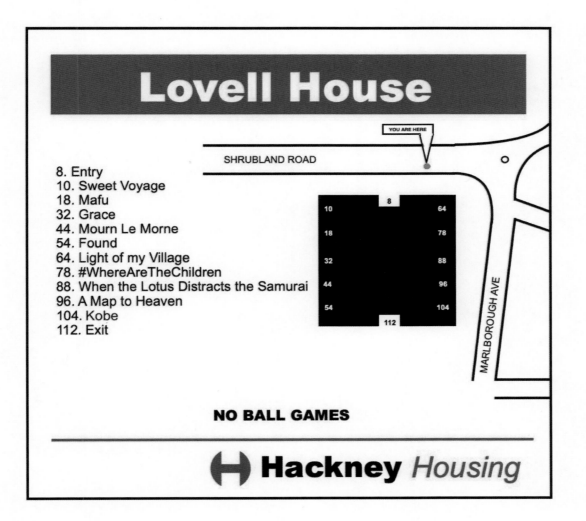

Lovell House

SHRUBLAND ROAD

YOU ARE HERE

MARLBOROUGH AVE

8. Entry
10. Sweet Voyage
18. Mafu
32. Grace
44. Mourn Le Morne
54. Found
64. Light of my Village
78. #WhereAreTheChildren
88. When the Lotus Distracts the Samurai
96. A Map to Heaven
104. Kobe
112. Exit

8
10
18
32
44
54
64
78
88
96
104
112

NO BALL GAMES

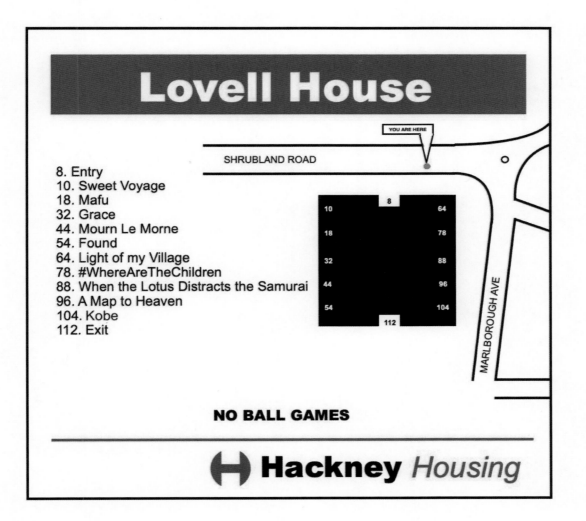 **Hackney** *Housing*

ENTRY

STORIES HEARD IN THE ESTATE

My mother often talks about our home country, an island in the Indian Ocean. She talks about the rich colours, the health-giving sun and the big-hearted people. She think's I can't relate, living as I do with England's shades of grey, heavy clouds and busy-busy society.

I can relate; I can understand. Lovell House is like an island. I sit and stare out of the window of our flat at the vehicles, swarming over the streets, covering them like the foam on the sea. The comparison is a good one because the attitude of London's drivers is quite salty. The high-rise buildings are like palm trees. The coconuts right at the top of the tree are hard to get to, but sweet and delicious and filled with sustenance when you do. Living here, we're all thirsty to get to the top.

My flat – my island – keeps me safe. It protects me from the lurking sharks and preying killer whales. It's lonely on this island, but the temptation to leave and strive for the delicious fruit is just one among the many dangers without its walls, and sometimes used as bait.

My island is looked down upon by the residents of the tall trees, the boastful birds. But we work hard here; we contribute to the environment and protect the reef. We bond as a community, even though we are from different parts of the globe.

So, I say to my mother, "Your island is in the Indian Ocean. My home is this London estate, my island is the tower-block of Lovell House."

SWEET VOYAGE

STORIES HEARD IN THE ESTATE

When I was small, my auntie Marianna would take me out in Lisbon. I didn't have much growing up; my parents were constantly working, so my auntie looked after me. As an only child, I craved attention and had an eagerness to learn. Auntie Marianna was the gatekeeper to every answer.

With a sweet smile and joyful soul, my auntie Marianna was a mother, a cook, a cleaner; but not a lot of people knew this about her. She was an adventurer, she was courageous, she was independent, and most of all, she knew how to live life to the full.

Children emulate the behaviour they see. As I grew up, whenever we were apart, I often pondered on what Auntie Marianna would do in any given situation. This reflection would normally determine my choice.

Saturday morning was the greatest time of the week.

"*Tia, tia*," I'd call, leaving my parents with barely a backward glance, running through the door, dragging my half-discarded jacket behind me.

"*Meu bem*, let's take this off," then Auntie Marianna would scoop me up and carry me around the kitchen, finishing the cooking or whatever she had been doing when I arrived. My parents would go off to work and this is when the adventure began. Auntie Marianna would take me upstairs and we would go through all her old pictures, journals and jewellery. She would tell me about the days of high adventure when she would travel across the globe, seeing different cultures, people and places.

"Where was your favourite place, *tia*?" I asked one day.

"That I'm going to show you today, but first, shall we pick some tomatoes from the garden for lunch?"

"Yeah!"

I'd let my imagination run far and free when I was a child. Auntie Marianna's garden became a jungle and we were on the hunt for food to survive in the wild. I would climb through the vines and sneak past the nettles, reaching in close to capture the rare tomatoes of Auntie Marianna's Amazon.

"I got one!" I'd shout over to her as she watered down the plants.

"Good work, Clara. Any more?"

The deeper I voyaged into the leaves, vines and bushes, the more limited my visibility of Auntie Marianna became. On the doorstep of the old shed, a dark, hairy spider was spinning his web in front of my face. I froze. The spider had pulled me out of the enjoyment of my imagination and brought me back to realty, to the presence of danger around every corner. I felt fear squeeze my chest and my eyes flicked from side to side, pleading with my body to wake up, but all that did was cause tears. The spider edged closer and closer to the tip of my nose. I tried to scream, but fear blocked all the sound in my throat.

Two gentle hands placed themselves around my waist and lifted me from harm's way.

"Clara, are you OK?" Auntie Marianna's eyes scanned me over. She reached down into the pocket of her woolly cardigan and took out my inhaler, placing it into my mouth and puffing life back into my lungs. "Come on, let's get you inside where it's warm. Then we can have lunch."

Even lunch with Auntie Marianna was creative. She would prepare the most amazing dishes, filled with flavour and nutrition. Today, she encouraged me to eat all my food as we would be going out to her favourite place later and we needed all the energy we could find.

We took the bus. I still didn't know where we were going, what Auntie Marianna's favourite destination was. Filled with excitement, she told me that right here in Lisbon there were actually three significant places. Today was going to be our greatest adventure yet.

We arrived at the Jerónimos Monastery. Auntie Marianna held my hand, taking me into the grounds of the monastery where the gardens are. I ran around with her chasing me, laughing and shouting; I'm not sure the monks and nuns would have approved, but Auntie Marianna had taught me the importance of smiling, laughing and being in the moment when visiting somewhere memorable.

"A memory is attached to a feeling, and if you can remember places with a smile, you'll have a lot of happy memories." She explained to me how this was a holy place and showed me the high ceilings rising towards the sky, the intricate detail carved into the walls and the beautiful patterned arches.

"Is this where the Princess lives?" I asked.

"Unfortunately not, Clara, but you could be the first Princess to set foot in here." Auntie Marianna always encouraged me to believe and wonder.

As we explored, she taught me the history of the Jerónimos Monastery and explained to me it had once had a secret that has now spread all over the world.

"It's not a very good secret then, *tia*," I said, confused.

"*Meu bem*, you will see. This secret belongs to the Portuguese. The world can try to take it from us, but we will always be the originators."

We continued our journey and ended up outside Pastéis de Belém, a large bakery café offering delicious local pastries.

"Hungry?" she asked. I nodded enthusiastically.

As we made our way inside, we were greeted by the waiting staff, wandering around between the blue-and-white tiled walls. Auntie Marianna told me the story of how the monks had sold a special recipe to Pastéis de Belém to earn a bit of money after the closure of the monastery in the aftermath of the Liberal Revolution in 1820. I was so excited, swinging our linked hands as we approached the counter where the patisserie chef awaited our orders. My aunt ordered two *pastel de nata* while I looked around at the many people coming into the café.

As the volume of people rose, I held on to my auntie's leg; the feeling of being overwhelmed by the crowd brought the fear into my chest again. As much as I tried to fight it off, I couldn't breathe.

I lost hold of Auntie Marianna's leg and slid down to the floor, sitting on her foot. She raised me up once again. With my eyes wide open, I could see her lips moving, but I couldn't hear a word she said.

Concentrating on her mouth and feeling the vibrations of her voice soothing my nerves, I slowly stopped panicking. As my aunt's soft voice steadily calmed me, I placed my hands on her beautiful saint-like face. When Auntie Marianna took me home that day after my panic attack, I slept while she sat close by, protecting me as always.

As the years passed, I grew up, grew older, but so did my aunt. I'd thought our adventures and our youth would last forever, but I was wrong. I never had a chance to visit the third significant place Auntie Marianna mentioned. She passed away in my late teenage years.

It was on a Saturday morning, once my favourite time of the week, that I found myself sorting through some of her stuff. I found a card I had written to her:

'To Auntie Marianna,

I hope you get better soon, and when you are well, come and visit me in my tower.

1 4

Love,

Princess Clara.'

I smiled at the memory, and it was then that I realised the third place Auntie Marianna would have taken me that day. I grabbed my stuff and headed straight out the door, taking a bus downtown.

The Belém Tower. I sat with it right in front of me and spoke the words I wanted to say to my aunt.

"I can only see the world for what it is because of the way you viewed it. The wrinkles in your skin were testament to many struggles, but the skin itself was soft and warm. The struggles may have shown on your face, but your ability to comfort me never waned. Your eyes consumed the horror and the dangers of the world, but as I glanced over to you, when you looked down at me, joy and love are all you allowed me to see.

"I wonder if the world can see and feel the way you did. I wonder if anyone else absorbs the hardships you did, but only allows their loved ones to see the beauty of life. I could sit here all day, remembering that the mere sight of you would always make the world better.

"As I search for your hand, the hand that should be have been here in mine, the wind mocks me, sweeping through and brushing my empty palm. Although you may be gone, this moment right here will always reflect and relate to you, Auntie Marianna."

I reached into my bag, took out a *pastel de nata* and enjoyed it, making this memory a happy one.

AUTHOR'S NOTES

'Sweet Voyage' is based on my wife's experience growing up. With her parents working, she was often left in the care of her auntie Maria.

I never met Maria, but my wife has told me all about her: her character, her joy and her spirit. I believe we all have people who come into our lives and subconsciously build our characters, and when they pass on, we're left with a part of them forever inside us. Sometimes our fears overpower our joy in the moment, but even with fear, a moment can still be memorable in a good way.

Clara ended her journey at The Belém Tower, enjoying a *pastel de nata* while remembering her auntie Marianna. This goes to show that when two people set out on a journey together, they can still complete it together, even when one person is no longer physically present.

STORIES HEARD IN THE ESTATE

MAFU

STORIES HEARD IN THE ESTATE

Here we go again, I thought. Only this time, it was different. My body quaked with adrenaline and nervousness; a familiar feeling, but today it was more intense. The butterflies raced around my insides. My heart pounded painfully against my chest, every beat vibrating my skin. The noise of the crowd charged my body, electrifying the hairs which stood up like an alert alley cat's tail.

The scared little boy in my head told me to stop. Not to go ahead tonight. He always visited me at moments like this. I needed him to leave.

The leather that protected my hands couldn't disguise the agitation my body felt. My knuckles grooved into the gloves and were ready for the violence that this night would bring. Most people work in an office or factory or shop to provide for their family; I risk my life to provide for mine.

After this evening, I would finally be able to see my beloved Melino. It had been five years.

"It's go time!" the backstage assistant shouted into the room.

"You ready, Kapo?" my coach asked me as he clamped his thick hands on to my shoulder. I nodded slightly as the nervousness reached my Adam's apple and muted my voice.

He began the prayer in his rusty voice.

"Oh, Almighty God!

You are our Lord.

It is You, the Pillar

And the Love of Tonga,

Look down on our prayer.

This is what we do now

May You answer our wish to protect us."

The prayer reminded me of my church back home.

I'm not a religious man, but I'm thankful to the Big Guy upstairs for blessing me with my beautiful wife and safe home.

I remembered our wedding, how Melino and I had taken our vows on a windy day at Uiha Island. This sacred place, where I promised I would love, protect and provide for her for the rest of my life, had once been the burial ground for royalty. There weren't a lot of people at the wedding, but the people who did come mattered.

As we walked out to the arena, sweat gathered under the wraps in my gloves. My body became unstable as my jitters peaked and sapped my fragile energy. I needed to snap out of this. It was wartime.

"Three, two, one," the assistant shouted as he pulled the curtain open. The music that began to play surged through my body, giving me a new lease of life. It soothed my nerves and allowed me to clear my head.

I could see myself back home in the summertime, serenading Melino as we walked down to the shopping mall, eating our ice creams. Melino was so timid, she would become as red as the Tongan flag as I sang to her.

"Stop, you're so embarrassing," she would say.

"Once I'm the champion of the world, we can get our own place. I can bring money into the community and we can start thinking about our little ones."

Melino disliked violence of any sort, but she knew this sport was my life. She understood that as much as she was my priority, I lived in the canvas ring.

"I love you, Kapo, you have the biggest heart." She'd blush again, reminding me of the myriad colours of the sky at sunset as my lips pressed onto her forehead.

The roar of the crowd was amplified as my body reached new heights. While I was walking to the ring, the little boy inside my head knew he had to face his demons tonight. We would not go down without a fight.

STORIES HEARD IN THE ESTATE

There were thousands in the audience, rippling like the waves of the sea, and they'd all come here tonight to watch me perform. There had been a time in my life when I'd been non-existent in society, just another gym rat trying to make it to the bright lights of Vegas. I was another statistic lost in the system, a young kid from the streets with a burning desire to make something of his life and escape from the criminality that surrounded him. Tonight, I had the world at my feet.

I climbed up to the ring and slipped through the ropes, bouncing around. I could lose part of my soul and gain another in here. In boxing, you put your mind, body and soul into every punch, but that means you could potentially lose all those parts of yourself when on the receiving end of a knockout blow.

I shook my arms and legs to loosen my body and remove all signs of the visit from the scared little boy. My opponent made his way to the ring as his music blared through the stadium. He had a sinister smile on his face, as did his crooked promoter.

Revenge lurked within me as I remembered all the years I'd missed with my wife and family. Kelvin Mayo, the slimy promoter who stood behind my opponent, was the same promoter who'd promised me so much from boxing, and it was all a scam to line his own pockets. I'd refused to agree to fights that were in the best interests of my opponents rather than myself. I was never going to throw a fight or sign a contract for money. This set me back because Mayo tarnished my reputation, declaring me to be a big ego. I was a risk to work with because I wasn't a yes man to the suits and ties. As much as I love this beautiful sport, there are always more than just the opponents in the ring.

The announcer took to the centre of the ring and brought the microphone to his clean-cut face.

"Ladies and gentlemen, welcome to the main event of the evening. With thousands in attendance and the whole world watching… let it begin!"

I strutted around the ring, looking past the announcer to my opponent. He was going to learn about a whole new world of pain tonight.

"Presenting the challenger from Nuku'alofa, weighing 246 pounds. With a perfect record of twenty-one victories and no defeats, he is the fighting pride of Tonga. Please welcome Kapo 'Showtime' Mafu!"

I'd earned the ring name 'Showtime' seven years ago when I'd knocked out Jimmy Rooks, a top prospect, within twenty seconds of the bell ringing.

"This next man needs no introduction. From Huntington Beach, California, USA, weighing 252 pounds, with a perfect record of thirty-five victories and no defeats, he is your reigning undefeated undisputed Heavyweight Champion of the World, Pablo 'El Segador' Garcia!"

Garcia's corner men raised his belt high, the gold glaring at me. I remembered that glare well. The piercing sun of Tonga. I missed home. Five years I had been bleeding, sweating and mourning, desperate to go back.

I wasn't academically gifted, so my father had invested his time in teaching me how to fight. He said we originated from the great warriors of Tonga. But the United States had become a prison after Kelvin Mayo had abandoned me. My trainers left me and my team moved to more financially stable fighters. Left with an eviction notice, I opted to train for fights rather than eat. I was stranded and couldn't go back home to my family; I had given my word to my people that when I returned, I would provide for our island. The glare of gold was the goal; the sun was my home.

The referee called us both to the centre of the ring and went over the rules. I stared into my opponent's deep brown eyes, into the abyss of his soul. He stood slightly taller and was heavier than me, but it wasn't necessarily enough for him to defeat me. As was expected in a man who'd competed in so many fights, he had scars and battle wounds all over his face. The most obvious was on his chin, only it wasn't from boxing. Pablo Garcia was notorious for having come up through a rough neighbourhood of LA. A blade had slit his throat when he was sixteen during an altercation, but he had fought his way out of the attack, all the while keeping pressure on his neck with one hand. Garcia had stared death in the face and he looked like a man who did not fear it. The bright lights didn't frighten him, nor did the demanding audience; he was ready.

Defeat for me would affect my family. Badly. Fear sometimes causes a person to run and cower, sometimes unleashes a wild animal.

Mafu, I said to myself, *your heart gives you the ability to fight when you think you can't fight any more. When you've taken all the punishment your body can endure, the soul is not ready to rest, so you get back up and you continue to fight.*

The referee uttered his last words before battle commenced. "If you wish to touch gloves, do so now." I bumped my gloves into Garcia's, mutual respect between warriors before brutality.

As I walked back to my corner, my eyes stayed locked on my opponent. *Ding, ding!* The bell rang, the action button. As I paced to the centre of the ring, my heels stayed off the ground, my toes remained pinned to the canvas. My hands shielded my face, ready to make contact. I extended my arm for a snappy jab, keeping my opponent at a distance. A few exchanges, but this first round was more of a waiting game as we assessed and felt our way into the fight.

The bell rang again and I returned to my corner, sitting on my stool. My corner men were speaking to me, but everything was so loud, I couldn't hear. I looked past my coach's shoulder to my opponent, who was staring at me like a hyena preying on his victim, his eyebrows overshadowing his fixated eyes. The cavity between his abdominals paved the way for the sweat dripping down his body and his shoulders were raised like a lion ready to pounce.

The ring girl came in and strutted around with her board. Melino hated this part of boxing even more than the violence, although she must know I would never look at any woman other than her. My father and her father had been best friends. Before we had even been born, they'd promised each other that their children would marry, keeping the families united. Naturally, I had argued against being a part of an arranged marriage, until I had thought about the proposal. I had known Melino my whole life. We had grown up together, played together and gone to school together. Melino was – and is – my best friend; marrying her was an honour, to myself and our families.

Ding, ding. Round Two had begun.

The nervousness had worn off; I glided around the ring, thriving in my battleground. I bobbed, weaved and ducked punches, but equally, my opponent was countering me, making me miss. A stern right hand had me tasting leather, throwing me off balance like a toddler gathering its feet. The crowd screamed. I was not hurt, just caught off guard. The referee watched closely, but I returned with a combination of punches; I was still in the contest.

The fight went on. It was pretty even until the sixth round. Then, I started gaining the better of my opponent, but it was still an all-out brawl. Haymakers and devastating punches were landing cleanly on both sides. I rocked him, sending him stumbling into the ropes. I approached further, but as he began to tire and fade, he brought his head down, colliding into me. A laceration to my right eye leaked blood, blurring my vision. I shielded my face with my gloves, protecting myself, then I was on the back foot, defending.

My opponent used this opportunity to go to work on my body. I neglected to protect it, sacrificing it to guard my wound from any more damage. He hacked away like a lumberjack, landing rib-crushing shots and potent liver punches.

Ding, ding! The bell rang for the end of the round. As I dropped my hands, Garcia hit me with a dirty shot, opening my wound. My face was now soaked in blood; that's all I could see, smell and taste. Blood. Thick and warm, salty and metallic, dripping into my mouth. I spat it out, trying to catch my breath.

The referee jumped between us and intervened. "Go back to your corner!" he shouted.

Garcia taunted me, smirking and laughing as he showboated back to his corner.

My head was throbbing as my corner men rushed inside the ring to work on my cut. The body shots had depleted my energy, my walk was heavy footed.

I've been here before, I thought. The long-distance runs at the break of dawn, the gruelling conditioning and the savage sparring; all were in preparation for this fight.

I stood up from my stool, ready to go into the seventh round. Garcia grinned at me mockingly, trying to throw me off my game. He wasn't going to lure me in; I was smarter than that. This was my ticket home, my family's future.

I boxed. Executing the sweet science of this brutal sport, I stayed light and agile on my toes as I hovered around the ring, keeping Garcia no less than arm's length as I let loose my venomous jabs, bobbing my head off his incoming punches. But the next few rounds started to take a toll on my body. His shots were slowing me down, leaving me out of gas sooner.

"We're down two rounds, Kapo, I need you to dig deep and bring us back," my coach said as I returned to my stool after the tenth round. This wasn't the first time I had been behind. I was behind my father the night he was killed. He was towing my vehicle after it had broken down on the highway. We were approaching a junction when a drunk driver skipped the red light and blind-sided him. My car swerved out of danger, but the collision wounded him fatally. If he had been five seconds ahead, it would have been me. I have thought about those five seconds every day since he died.

"Five seconds, that's all I need," I muttered to myself. My coach squeezed the sponge of cold water over my shoulders and looked at me in concern.

I allowed Garcia to believe I was starting this round cautiously and let him come to me. I ducked down, faking a shot to the body, and followed that up with an overhand right to his cranium. A gash opened up under his left eye as I cornered him, throwing combinations of punches to capitalise on his wound. Even with the finishing line in sight, every shot was a risk as my body fatigued.

One shot. One shot was all it took to my gut and down I went.

"One…"

I have been down before. I lost everything: my home, my financial stability, my father.

"Two…"

I've been away from my soulmate for five years, and part of my soul has departed my body during this fight.

"Three…"

I have bled for this sport, for these people, for this money. But really, I bled for my family and my land.

"Four…"

It's time I went back home. I am the son of Tonga. I belong where the blazing sun rises and the ocean sings to the waves of Polynesia.

"Five..."

Mafu, have heart. When your body is at its limit, when your soul has split and part of it has departed, when your blood has paid its debt, your heart can raise you to your feet and allow you to become immortal.

The sounds of the crowd were muffled in my ears as I stood in a limbo between life and death. My opponent refused to believe I was able to fight, buying me time to gather my consciousness. The referee looked at me cautiously, asking me to move forward, showing I could continue to fight. He clapped his hands for the fighting to resume, but as I limped forward, the bell rang. The eleventh round ended.

I stumbled to my stool, dazed. My ears were ringing and my vision was limited.

"What on earth are you doing out there?" my coach screamed at me. "I'm throwing in the towel. That's enough, Kapo. I can't watch you do this anymore."

"No!" I forced the words out as my gum shield fell to the floor. "I got him! Coach, this is my time. This is my way home." I ripped the towel from his hand, chucked it into the crowd and turned to face my opponent for Round Twelve.

"Please, God, can you hear me? Bless my family and take me home." Those were my father's last words before he passed away in my arms. I was prepared to gamble with death to go home tonight.

I screamed, pounding my chest. My gloves acting as a defibrillator, I moved forward, planting my feet on the canvas; I was grounded. With every step, I exhaled heavily. I had practised this manoeuvre excessively in training over many days, weeks, months and years. Fake the right-hook to the head, turn my body downward, use the momentum to swing a bouldering shot to the ribs followed by an uppercut directly to the chin. Garcia's body became floppy, his eyes closed and he collapsed to the floor of the ring.

"One…"

No response.

"Two…"

Nothing.

"Three…"

Garcia palmed his gloves to the floor.

"Four…"

He started to sit up.

"Five…"

He planted his foot down, kneeling up.

"Six…"

He wobbled on to his feet, still bent over.

"Seven…"

He stood straight.

"Eight…"

The referee requested him to come forward.

"Nine…"

He raised his gloves up and stepped forward. My lungs expanded, pushing my ribs outwards as I inhaled this moment: the wide eyes and gaping mouths of Garcia's corner men; the deafening noise of the crowd piercing my eardrums; the back of my neck prickling with sweat.

There wasn't a ten count. As Garcia stepped forward, he fell back down, losing his balance. The referee waved the fight finished.

STORIES HEARD IN THE ESTATE

I dropped to my knees. "Mafu," I whispered, "you're going home."

AUTHOR'S NOTES

'Mafu' was originally published in *TOKEN* magazine, issue 4, and I would like to give thanks to the team at *TOKEN* for making this story a part of their collection. The sport of boxing has been important in my life and has taught me so much from a young age, so I wanted to showcase the feelings and emotions a fighter experiences in the lead up to a fight and during the walk to the ring. The buzz is beyond comprehension.

Polynesian culture has always fascinated me. As a son of island people, I take a keen interest in other small island cultures, as you will see throughout this collection. Tonga has a long history of warriors, so making Kapo Mafu a fighter who's trying to get back home to that island became my main focus.

I also wanted to touch on his history, his relationships with his father and wife. Boxers tend to be very emotional and passionate people; we don't fight for nothing. No-one does anything without a reason.

Finally, I wanted to touch briefly on the crooked system that still goes on today within the boxing industry and the combat world. A fighter is not just fighting their opponent in the ring; they have many obstacles in the form of training, weight cutting, promoters, travelling, not to mention personal issues.

A fighter is a noble title to have. A fighter shows great discipline and commitment, and I have much respect and love for the life. Although it's a lonely journey, a fighter's dreams are often both simple and deep.

STORIES HEARD IN THE ESTATE

GRACE

STORIES HEARD IN THE ESTATE

A chilly morning saw an elderly man waiting outside his country home for a taxi. Exhaling his warm breath into the cold air, he produced a fine mist all around him. The mist settled and glazed over the small poppy, pinned with pride to the lapel of his jacket.

He stood waiting. The cold attacked him, pinching the loose skin on his hands, forcing him to put them in his pocket where a scrunched-up tissue comforted them with warmth.

The date was the eleventh of November, a day to remember.

The taxi pulled up in front of the elderly man and he reached for the back door handle. Pausing, he looked over the roof of the vehicle.

"You OK there, Mr Westcarr?" the driver said from behind the steering window.

"Yes, of course." He opened the car door and sat on the slippery leather seat, adjusting his seatbelt.

"Good morning, Mr Westcarr, sir, how are you?" the driver asked.

"Good morning, Richie, I am well, thank you." Rubbing his hands, spreading the warmth around his palms and fingers, Mr Westcarr leant back into his seat and tried to relax for his journey. His head pressed against the restraint, he turned it to the right, staring out the car window. His warm breath tried escaping into the air, but became trapped against the glass.

Mr Westcarr rubbed his palm along the glass. Removing the condensation, he looked up into the sky above the family homes as the taxi passed them by, watching the birds flying in formation. The way they dived and swooped just before they crashed into the roofs reminded him of something. He swallowed a surge of nervousness.

The elderly man reached his trembling hands out to the seat next to him.

"Mr Westcarr, are you OK back there?" The driver looked into his rear-view mirror.

"Yes, I'm quite alright, Richie. Do you have some water I could trouble you for?" His fingers shook further as he tried to stroke his neck.

"Of course," the driver passed a bottle to Mr Westcarr. The elderly man sipped the water and sighed, trying to digest an almost forgotten memory. It seemed harder for him to soothe the pain this year.

"Richie, is it possible to put the radio on, please?" Mr Westcarr started to lean forward, but the seatbelt restricted him.

"Of course, sir."

"*Today marks the anniversary of the end of World War I.*" A woman's voice spoke from the radio. "*We honour and salute the veterans of both World Wars for their bravery and courage. We will remember them.*"

Mr Westcarr adjusted his cufflinks as the beeping of the radio dragged him into a nightmare that reoccurred on this day every year. He tapped his finger along the window in time to the beeps, almost as if he was receiving a message in Morse code. He remembered the short beeps, the long beeps and the spaces of silence in between; the pencil he had scratched across the thin, grainy white paper, scribing the message:

'--. --- --- -.. -... -.-- . / -... .-. --- - .... . .-. --..-- / .. / .-.. --- ...- . / -.-- --- ..- .-.-.-'

'*GOODBYE/BROTHER/I/LOVE/YOU.*'

White noise awoke him from his nightmare as sweat beaded on the surface of his skin. He dabbed it away, catching Richie's attention in the rear-view mirror.

"I'm so sorry about that, Mr Westcarr, let me turn that off and open the window for you." The driver panicked, pressing a bunch of buttons until the windows opened.

"Thank you, Richie." The fresh, cold air breezed into Mr Westcarr's face. He closed his eyes, squeezing his eyelids tight shut in the hope of erasing this nightmare for today.

Mr Westcarr opened his eyes to the sound of a child running along the pavement as the car came to a halt at traffic lights. A young boy with a superhero mask covering his face was laughing and giggling as he was chased by his father. The mask caught the elderly man's attention as he squinted his eyes, gawking at the little boy.

He remembered running across London's streets with a group of young children, all wearing gas masks. The terror of looking above weighed heavily against the back of his cranium. That day, as bombers divided the skies, dropping their evil cargo and destroying British soil, a young boy fell while running for shelter and Mr Westcarr had turned back. As he looked down at the boy before picking him up, the lens in his gas mask had shown the reflection of explosives pouring to the ground. Behind this reflection, fear dripped onto the protective glass, an image Mr Westcarr found hard to forget. So much pain and horror still lived on in this veteran's life.

"Pardon me, Richie, but will we be much longer?" Mr Westcarr leaned back onto the headrest.

"No, not at all, sir, we have just arrived." The driver pulled up alongside the front of the restaurant and parked.

Mr Westcarr opened the car door. "Thank you, Richie. Goodbye for now."

"Bye, Mr Westcarr."

Mr Westcarr approached the big glass double doors of the restaurant. Pushing one side open, he left condensation from the heat of his hand on its surface. He entered the restaurant and was greeted by the front of house.

"Good morning, Mr Westcarr, if you would like to wait at the bar, we will notify you when your table is ready."

"Oh, good morning. Yes, that would be grand." Going in the direction the woman at the front desk had gestured with her hand, Mr Westcarr sat on a stool at the bar and leaned forward onto the white marble counter. He brushed his left shirt sleeve up and looked down at his watch. The little silver hand was a minute away from eleven o'clock.

Live on the television, a wounded soldier read *The Exhortation*, which began the two minutes of silence.

"They shall grow not old, as we that are left grow old,
Age shall not weary them, nor the years condemn.
At the going down of the sun and in the morning,
We will remember them."
We will remember them.

Mr Westcarr bowed his head out of respect, finding the silver band on his ring finger with his thumb. He rubbed his thumb across the band; the print of his skin pressed against the scratches and grazes in the silver. The marks of his cherished memories. He found comfort in the dented edges and uneven curve.

The playing of *Reveille* signalled the end of the silence.

"Excuse me, sir, would you like to follow me to your table?" Mr Westcarr raised his head and walked behind the waitress, passing the other customers. Families, couples and friends, all dining together and enjoying each other's company. The restaurant's big arched windows never failed to astonish and surprise Mr Westcarr. He stood in awe, staring out at the world before he took his seat.

The pianist was playing a fine melody, soothing the atmosphere of the restaurant. A table for two had been set up for Mr Westcarr; his regular spot. St

Paul's Church across the road brought a sad smile to his face. A place filled with many celebrations and much love, this church had been the beginning of a journey for Mr Westcarr, but also the end of a chapter.

"Would you like to see the set lunch menu, Mr Westcarr?" A familiar voice brushed over his right shoulder. He turned, looking up to the gentleman standing behind him.

"Ah, Robert. How are you, young sir?" He held his hand out and the waiter shook it.

"I am very well, thank you. It's always a pleasure to see you." Robert smiled as he released Mr Westcarr's hand.

"Yes please, Robert, the set menu would be lovely." Mr Westcarr placed the menu on the table and searched his inner pocket for his glasses, placing the frame on his nose and looking down through them. "I will have the parsnip and apple soup, followed by the steak, medium to well done."

Robert was scribbling on his notepad. "And to drink?"

"Water will do."

As Mr Westcarr took his glasses off, Robert repeated the order back to him.

"And will sir be having dessert?"

"Maybe so, we shall see." Mr Westcarr chuckled, rubbing the bottom of his nose.

The waiter, Robert, made his way back to the bar and Mr Westcarr sighed in relief. He glanced over at the chair in front of him, adoring the sight for a moment, then Robert returned, placing a small plate of bread and a spoon for the soup on the table. The elderly man rubbed the warmth into his hands as he began to relax.

A white ceramic bowl was placed onto the plate in front of Mr Westcarr. A faint smell of onion and garlic rose with the warm vapours of the soup; the fresh scent of creamy parsnips lingered in the nostrils; the sweet aroma of Bramley apples bedded down on his tongue, causing him to salivate. Apples always reminded him of the tree in his garden. In the late summertime, Mr Westcarr and his wife would pick the apples from the tree, then Mrs Westcarr would spend the afternoon baking an apple pie. He smiled at the thought of an apple bringing him such a joyful moment.

A painting to his right caught Mr Westcarr's attention. It was an image against a blue background of a person sitting with their back to the restaurant. He sat, pondering over what it could mean, neither in adoration nor in criticism. Wondering what the person in the painting was looking at, or not looking at, he sipped his water again, gazing at the other side of the table. His shoulders stooped lower as he relaxed even more.

The main course followed. A chestnut-brown piece of meat, a succulent six-ounce sirloin steak with the perfect grill lines on the surface of the flesh, dominated the plate, accompanied by crispy golden homemade chips. A beautiful green side salad rested under half a bright yellow lemon.

Mr Westcarr recalled the many times his wife insisted he eat more greens. *"Oh, Errol, all that meat is no good for you. Please eat more veg,"* she would say, overloading his plate with salad. Mr Westcarr enjoyed being fussed over by his wife, he liked the attention.

He chuckled while squeezing the lemon over his greens. "I'm eating them now, darling," he whispered.

"How was the food, sir?" the waiter asked as he began clearing the table.

"It was splendid, Robert, a memorable treat," Mr Westcarr said as he dabbed his napkin on his mouth.

STORIES HEARD IN THE ESTATE

"How about that dessert menu?"

The elderly man smiled. "Desert would be wonderful."

"Here it is." The waiter produced the menu from behind his back. "I'll give you five minutes."

As Mr Westcarr looked through the desserts, he noticed a familiar treat he had always loved. It was a special dish that he did not have often, usually just on birthdays. Mrs Westcarr would bake the pudding the night before and hide it, playfully tricking him into believing she had forgotten. After dinner, she would come into the front room with a beaming smile while he was relaxing in front of the fire, waving a plate of soft, rich, delicious surprise.

"Bread and butter pudding, sir?" The waiter was back.

"She used to…" Mr Westcarr paused, his eyes wandering over to the chair opposite him again, trying to find comfort in an empty space.

"Mr Westcarr, it's one of our best desserts," Robert persisted. "Mr Westcarr?"

He snapped out of his daydreaming. "Oh, yes, yes, of course. Bread and butter pudding would be marvellous."

Overwhelmed with emotions, Mr Westcarr felt himself twitch and become agitated. Although all this wonderful food brought back some cherished memories, it also reminded him of something he was not ready to let go of.

He pushed the chair back and began to stand.

"Oh, Mr Westcarr, I don't think you would want to go anywhere just yet," Robert said as he placed the pudding onto the table.

"I… It smells and looks great."

"It is, wait until you try it."

Mr Westcarr sat back down. He parted a piece of the pudding with his spoon, placing it into his mouth. The caramelised sugar on the baked bread caused his mouth to water. The fluffy texture of the milky treat soaked into his taste buds. The occasional hint of cinnamon partnered with sultanas enhanced the sweetness with a natural flavour.

Finishing the dessert, Mr Westcarr placed the spoon down in satisfaction, raising his glass of water to swirl the luxury indulgence down his throat.

"Oh, Grace, you would have enjoyed that," he said to the chair opposite him.

"Mr Westcarr, how was the food?" Robert asked as he cleared the table once again.

"It was delightful, I really enjoyed it all." Mr Westcarr produced a big smile.

"We have one more thing for you, sir." The waiter handed him a card.

"Oh, thank you," Mr Westcarr said. Baffled, he opened the envelope. A card with two ducks on the front read:

'Dear Mr Westcarr,

Thank you for your service during wartime, without which we would not be here today.

Although today is Remembrance Day, a day of great importance to us all, it is also your anniversary.

We miss Grace too.

You will always have a table in our restaurant on the most important day of your life, and today, lunch is on us.

With best wishes, from everyone at the restaurant.'

STORIES HEARD IN THE ESTATE

AUTHOR'S NOTES

'Grace' was originally submitted to a short-story competition, in which it did not place. The competition's writing prompt was to include food in the story, so I had the idea of a gentleman who goes to the same restaurant every year with his wife Grace to celebrate their anniversary, only this year's different.

When I began writing this, I thought about how cold November is in England. I wanted to embody the bleakness and the temperature of the month in my words, giving the reader a feel of the time of year. Playing on the solemnity of Remembrance Day and Mr Westcarr's history as a World War II veteran, I also wanted to highlight some of the trauma that such people lived with after the war.

The switch in the story comes with the memories evoked by the wedding band and the long pauses as Mr Westcarr stares at the chair opposite him in the restaurant. Memories are a vital part of being human; we remember parts and people in our lives from smells, taste and imagery. A certain scent, a certain taste associated with a memory, a familiar place – all hold shadows from the past.

I used the surname 'Westcarr' in honour of a former work colleague. I often spoke to him about my stories and ideas, and he told me about his culture, history and family. I cherish people like that. This story is dedicated to all African, Caribbean and Asian soldiers who fought in the war.

We work so hard in life, but often forget *why* we're working so hard. Create memories, be in the moment, because one day, looking back, you'll want to be able to smile on the bank of the river of remembrance, knowing that it's more than just water and soil.

STORIES HEARD IN THE ESTATE

MOURN LE MORNE

STORIES HEARD IN THE ESTATE

On a wet Tuesday after school, I'd just finished scavenging in the cupboards for some snacks and was running up to my room to consume the evidence before my mum came home.

"Ad!" I heard my dad calling me from downstairs. I scampered out of my bedroom and leant over the bannisters at the top of the stairs. "Put your shoes on, I'll drop you off at Uncle Fazel's on my way to the gym."

I wiped the crumbs off my face and skipped down the stairs two at a time in excitement, wedging my feet into my shoes and sprouting my arms through the sleeves of my puffer jacket.

"You ready, boy?" Dad said, placing his hand out for me to hold.

I smiled. "Yeah."

While walking to my uncle's house, my dad took long strides and I had the task of pacing myself to keep up with him. When we arrived at my uncle's, Fazel opened the door to us and greeted us. My dad asked him to watch over me while he worked out at the gym for an hour or so.

My uncle muttered through his boiled sweet and wiry beard, "You alright, boy? Abu is playing on the computer."

I nodded and kicked off my shoes and flung my jacket on the bannister. After saying bye to my dad, I darted towards the stairs, crawling up the steps like a monkey, filled with joy at the thought of seeing my cousin.

"Boo-Boo, what you playing?" I said, entering the room.

"*Golden Axe*, want to play?" Abu passed me a controller and I hopped up on to his air hockey table which was inches away from the television. It felt like he was hours into gameplay, beating up bad guys and advancing levels.

I pressed 'Start', pausing the game. "I need a wee-wee," I said, sliding down off the hockey table.

Abu shooed me away. "Hurry, we have two more levels to get to the boss."

I opened his bedroom door and stepped onto the landing, making me fair game for all the monsters in the dark. The dark scared me, as I could not see what was lurking in the shadows. I gripped onto the bannister and crept down the stairs, being careful not to alert the monsters. My uncle Fazel was in the spare room; I could see the light peeping out from the edge of the doorway. It was my beacon of light and safe haven if I needed to turn back.

I walked past in stealth mode, keeping the monsters at bay. Making my way to the kitchen, I hit the light switch and ran as fast as I could to the toilet. The monsters were now inches away from my back.

Finally, despite all the adrenaline and nervousness, I could wee. I was extra careful; my auntie Sakeena would have put the bamboo stick to my backside if I wasn't.

A sudden flash illuminated the restroom as I flushed. *What was that?* I thought. A loud clatter followed by a violent rumble sounded from outside. I needed to get back upstairs; the monsters were lurking again.

As I opened the toilet door, I heard Abu's cat Ginger crying. He only had three legs; I couldn't leave him outside in the rain. I puffed out my chest and frowned my brave face on, opening the door.

Ginger stood by a patch of burnt grass.

"Come on, boy, get away from there," I whispered, tiptoeing over to him, doing my best to avoid the burnt grass. As I extended my arms to pick him up, he hopped away and I wobbled off balance, landing on the burnt patch. A charge of light and electricity struck me, elevating me into the sky. Ascending, I was in shock. My vision faded into darkness, my sight was lost. I awoke to pins and needles all over my body. Anchored to the ground, I could not move. The sound of a voice speaking a foreign language greeted my ears. Someone picked me up in well-worked arms, carrying me to what looked like a stable. My head knocked into the sugar canes as he took me towards my refuge.

"Where did you come from, boy?" At least, that's what I think he said, but I couldn't make out the words. The man was dark-skinned. He had a metal collar around his neck and shackles locked on to his wrists. My lips were stuck together and I couldn't reply. I managed to wiggle my toes; the feeling was coming back to my body, but I was still in shock.

It was late. The well-built dark-skinned man left me to rest on a bed in his stable. I could hear people coming and going around me, all whispering. I managed to palm my hands onto the bed, lifting myself up. I still didn't feel great, but I could cope.

A group of people had gathered around me.

"Boy, you are awake," said my rescuer, kneeling down beside where I lay. "I am Jean Phillipe. These people here are all slaves, but we long for our freedom. How did you get into this plantation?"

"I… I'm Adu. I don't know… I want to go home." My nose fizzled and my eyes became teary. A large lady wearing a headscarf stooped down, pulling me into her chest, comforting me.

"Adu, I'm Rosemary. Jean Phillipe is my husband. We will get you home."

The people who Jean Phillipe had introduced as slaves gathered together a few items, and then Jean Phillipe himself approached me. He offered me his hand to hold, much like my father did.

"We leave now," he whispered. I crept out of the barn with the slaves and walked past some high fences, a big house looming from the darkness a short way away from us. A loud bark echoed through the crisp air of the morning and the lights of the big house started to glow, flickering like candles caught in a breeze.

"Run!" Jean Phillipe said as I gripped his fingers tightly in mine.

As we ran, I could hear people shouting from the big house. The dogs I could hear barking approached, and then gunshots clattered and rumbled through the night. It reminded me of the thunder back in my uncle's garden.

I was petrified; I didn't know what was going to happen next. Screams of pain came from the tormented slaves; they were being shot and killed. Jean Phillipe was beginning to pant and tire.

"Don't stop, please don't stop," I begged.

I lost sight of Rosemary as Jean Phillipe picked his pace up.

"Rosemary?" I enquired. He turned his neck, looking back, and came to a halt. Releasing my hand and falling to his knees, Jean Phillipe crawled back towards his wife's lifeless body. The barks and the candles were drawing ever closer, so I ran. I ran as if all the monsters of the darkness were gaining ground on me, trying to catch up with the escaping slaves.

"Wait for me!" I shouted. The slave at the back of the group looked over his shoulder, noticing me galloping towards him. He stopped and swooped me up onto his back.

"Adu, where is Jean Phillipe?" he asked. I began crying at this horror, this nightmare. I just wanted to go home.

We travelled for a day until we reached a rugged mountain called Le Morne, a sanctuary and refuge for all runaway slaves. We were safe. There were hundreds of people on the mountain. Pascal, the slave who had carried me to freedom, introduced me to the others in his group, even though I found it difficult to understand the words he was saying.

"It's the Creole language," he told me in broken English. "It's actually a mix of various languages: African and South Asian dialects, as well as French."

The slaves were fun. It didn't matter that I didn't understand all they said; humour and high spirits don't worry about the boundaries of language. And I felt comfortable with them. There was something familiar about them, something that made me feel as if I belonged as we danced and sang 'Sega', which Pascal told me narrates the story of the slaves, their homes, their uprising and bravery.

Pascal also talked about the suffering of the slaves during their captivity. "There were days when the heat of the sun was too intense. But the best thing about the heat was it brought out the caramelised smell of the fields. I don't know what it was about that sweet aroma, but it uplifted my spirits. It gave me hope for tomorrow.

"I'd chant and sing when the slave masters weren't passing on their watch: *'Rich from the earth, stolen from my land'*. When the heat was unbearable, I would try my best to hide in the shade. The humidity would pinch the surface of my skin, making her cry and soak with sweat. Every day was hard labour, but on those days when the sun flew too close, the heat would crystallise the residue of sugar on my wet skin. I lived for those painful but beautiful moments in this life of terror. *A sweet freedom, sweet life I dream.*"

Pascal's eyes glazed over as he stared into the sun sinking on the horizon.

"Did the slave masters not scare you?" I asked.

"The slave masters could never destroy our spirit." I rested my head on Pascal's shoulder. Despite his friendship, despite loving the company of his people, despite the strange tug of familiarity in this foreign land, I felt alone.

"Pascal, I want to go home," I said as we sat on the beach, looking up at the mountain.

"We all want to go home, Adu, but this is our home now," he replied.

It was then that a shout came from one of the slaves. "*Allez! La police! Allez, la police!*" The colonisers had found us. Everyone began to panic. Pascal and I froze in shock, witnessing the slaves' escape plan as they leapt to eternal freedom from the mountainside. Death was a greater liberty than returning to chains.

The slave masters rushed up to what had once been a safe haven in an attempt to stop the slaves.

"*Allez,* Adu, *degasser, garçon.*"

At Pascal's command, I jumped into a fishing boat and he pushed me as far as he could out to sea. I expected him to get into the boat with me. He didn't.

"Pascal! Don't leave me!"

He didn't turn back. As the slaves were jumping to their deaths, I rowed the boat out into the unknown.

Lost at sea, I was cold and starving. I thought about jumping into the ocean to end my misery. I wanted to be at peace, but as I stared at my reflection in the mirroring water, I wanted to go home more than anything.

A storm whipped up from nowhere and tears drowned my boat. Thunder roared down at me and an electrifying light took hold of my hand, ascending me into the clouds.

Then, I was back in my uncle's garden.

"Ad?" My dad was standing at the front door. "You ready, boy?"

I nodded.

STORIES HEARD IN THE ESTATE

"Dad, where did our family come from?" I asked as we walked home, looking up at him. There was no metal collar around his neck. Why did I think there would be?

"We are from a little island in the Indian Ocean called Mauritius."

I looked at him, bewildered. "So how did we end up in England?"

'Imagine your people had a plan, and you were the way out.'

AUTHOR'S NOTES

My good friend Robert Kier initially gave me the idea of creating a collection of short stories. I submitted this story to a local competition, and even though it didn't place, I remember Rob encouraging me to keep writing. Rob loves Stephen King, so I'm sure his idea for me was inspired by that great author's work.

When I was a child, my dad would often drop me off at my uncle Fazel's house on the way to the gym. My father is an old-school gym goer; think Rocky in a weightlifting gym, somewhere old, damp and filled with guys training in torn clothes and workwear. My father knew that it wouldn't be a good idea to take me there as I would probably get up to no good, so he opted to leave me with my uncle.

My cousin Abu is the same age as me. We went to school together and were really close growing up, spending hours playing on his Sega Mega Drive: *Sonic*, *Streets of Rage* and *Golden Axe*. I did used to think monsters would come at me from the dark, so I developed a habit of running to and from places, not thinking to turn a light on.

Mauritius, my home country, the place where my family originates from, has a dark past. Part of me always ponders on the history of slavery and the stories that have come out of it. Although my story is fiction, Le Morne and its history are very real, so it's a fictional story based around a real event, if you like. Because its history is interlinked with that of my people, it does make me emotional when I think about the horror they went through, and I feel it's important to share their stories, our history.

While I was writing this story, transporting me as a child back to Mauritius in the time of slavery and experiencing a glimpse of life with the runaway slaves, I repeatedly felt that I just wanted to go home. As a child, when you are somewhere you don't know and you've lost sight of your parents, all you want to do is go home. Then I started thinking that was probably how the slaves would have felt, having been stolen from their homeland and brought to a country that was completely foreign to them. All they would have wanted to do was go home to their loved ones.

It is vital to know where we have come from so we can know where we are going. This is not just for us, but for our future generations, too.

FOUND

A woman stares past the shielding trees onto the whitish sand and glistering sea. Invisible, the modern world prohibited to her, she can only sit and watch, fantasising about what might have been.

A deep inhale and a disgruntled sigh. Picking up the basket of fruits she's collected for today's meal, she strolls back home.

"Josia, where have you been?" her sister's voice – the only friendly voice she ever hears these days – greets her as she enters the village.

"Nowhere but somewhere; somewhere but not near; near but far."

"Why do you always talk in riddles? You have been at the border again, haven't you?"

"Shh, be quiet! Mother will be angry if she hears you say that."

The two women walk home and begin preparing the food. But Josia's mind isn't on the job; it is where it always is: nowhere but somewhere; somewhere but not near; near but far. The beaches and highlands she knows so well, but in a happier time.

A time before Rahul.

Josia, the elder of two sisters, was a year away from marriage. Something she was frightened of. Something she didn't have a choice over. But that was the norm in her village. Josia was not the norm; she dreamed constantly about the outside world, about the wonders of a life unknown and alien to her people. She had spent all of her seventeen years of life in the Carib-Alogn territory, a community that wilfully cut itself off from the modern world and adhered rigidly to the customs and traditions that had been passed down over the centuries, from mother to daughter, father to son. She knew little of the surrounding islands, let alone the mysteries that lay beyond the vast blue-and-green ocean. But there was no intrigue in her world; no danger to fear; no passion in the known.

Most evenings, when Josia could, she would get away from the village and sit on the border with the *other* world. She would stare down at the beach from a distance, wondering what life would be like in the unknown. Before she fell asleep under the stars, she would ponder the great depths of space, longing to explore, to be lost, to be discovered.

And one night, Josia's fortune changed.

"Hey, you can't be here!" Josia whispered the first words that popped into her head upon waking. A pale face glanced back at her, light brown hair ruffled by the breeze, before the stranger returned his attention to the stars. But not before Josia had noticed his eyes. Green eyes. Not deep brown, like those of everyone she had ever known, but glittering green like the depths of the ocean. The most beautiful eyes she had ever seen.

As if reading her thoughts, the stranger began, "They're beaut..." then paused abruptly, looking down at the young woman. Her dark hair was silky in the light of the moon. Her enormous round eyes seemed to hold the wisdom of the world, secluded by the wilderness.

"I... I'm... my name is Rahul," he stuttered.

"You must leave, Rahul. This is the Carib-Alogn territory and you cannot be here."

As Rahul argued that the land belongs to all, Josia remained silent, listening. She was enthralled by this man. His clothes, speech, ideology on life were unlike anything she had experienced before. Rahul described the stars and their names. She had never heard these names. She'd never met anyone who had explored the depths of the astral world as he had.

"How do you know so much about them?' She pointed into the abyss of the night sky.

"I have been there. I have travelled past the stars and walked along the moon." Rahul offered his hand to Josia and she stood. "But I have barely seen a speck of the galaxy. Yet you are on the brink of discovering the unknown imprisoned in your eyes."

Josia looked down. She was standing a foot away from stepping out of the Carib-Alogn territory, led by this man of the sky. Her craving to discover the unknown world consumed her. She raised her bare foot; her sole was inches away from the forbidden earth.

The thrill Josia felt as she stepped into the new world overwhelmed her. Her forbidden journey had begun. Rahul led her down to the coast, their feet sinking into the wet sand from the late tide.

"I am lost for words, Rahul, how will I ever thank you for encouraging my dream?" Josia's senses heightened with excitement as she realised all of the magnificent things around her.

"You don't have to thank me, I am but a traveller passing through. My only request is for you to live in the moment, love from your soul and be the Josia you wish to be."

"What is love?" she asked, intrigued.

"Love is an addiction, but also a curse."

"Do I have love?" She tilted her head closer to his.

"Will it hurt going back to your village?"

"I have to go back…"

"So, love for tonight, as tomorrow is not promised."

Rahul painted the many wonders of the world with his words. His descriptions captivated Josia with the beauty of the unseen. They talked, laughed and taught each other about their lives. And they made love, the wandering village girl and the cosmic traveller. This was another first for Josia. Love overruled her common sense tonight. She was not ready for love to end; she wanted to love forever. She wanted to experience love with Rahul.

The birth of the new dawn awoke Josia. She stumbled around the room, picking up her robe, knocking into luggage.

"I need to go get the food for the village."

"Josia, wait…"

"I can't, I'll see you soon."

That evening, Josia couldn't wait to meet Rahul again. Devouring her food like a wild boar, she rushed out of the village, disregarding the rest of her duties. She ran part of her journey until the air weighed heavily on her chest, then she trekked, exhilarated by the thought of being loved again. Finally, she arrived at the border.

Looking down at the silent sea reflecting the stars, she waited – waited for Rahul and for love. The following two nights, she repeated her journey in hope of seeing Rahul and feeling his love again. But he didn't come. She was alone, something she had never felt before. She was hurt, something she'd never feared before, and she felt cursed. Cursed because she was addicted to love, but love had worked against her. Josia wept as she made her way back to the village, to what she knew. She never wanted to experience love again.

STORIES HEARD IN THE ESTATE

The waves stroke the sleeping shores, illuminated only by the moon, as a lonely woman stands watching. Many years have passed since Josia lay with the stranger from the skies. Many years since her body swelled to contain the boy child growing within her. For many years, she has been shamed and scorned, mocked by her people and shunned by the menfolk. She is unclean. She is impure. And when a light-skinned and green-eyed boy was born into this closed community, betraying her brief escape into a forbidden world, she had been forced to make an agonising decision that haunts her to this day.

Josia can still remember the screams of her baby boy as the ink man plunged sharpened bone into his delicate skin, marking him as one of the people of the village. Yet the child could never be so. He didn't look the same. He wasn't the same. He belonged to the wider world, not to the confines of the Carib-Alogn. And so Josia made the heartbreaking decision to give her baby back to the world to which he belonged.

"Forgive me, for I was not capable of being your guardian," she whispers into the still night air, as she has done every day since she kissed her infant son goodbye. "If God willed it and you have lived, one day, the symbol on your forearm will identify who you are and you will know where you belong. I love you, my son."

As the sun begins to change shifts with the moon, Josia's eyes glaze with sorrow. There are no words in this unforgiving world to explain how she feels, how hard her choice was. Blinking back her tears, she takes one last look out to sea, then turns to go back to her village. Yet deep in her heart, she knows that he will return. One day, she will stand at the border, and a young man will rush into the loving arms of his mother. And until that day dawns, she will wait. She will wait for as long as it takes.

AUTHOR'S NOTES

'Found' was created as a companion to my 2020 novella, *Escape*. Even when I decided I was done with the writing of *Escape*, something still didn't sit well with me. There were too many unanswered questions.

Josia's story of finding one's self in the unknown is something many people can relate to. I think a lot of us live with the mindset of island life, where we are afraid to try something new. We allow our minds to wander, but never allow our bodies to action our thoughts.

Although in some cases, we can make mistakes when we venture out into something new, mistakes are a part of life. In Joisa's case, we can question which part is the mistake. Leaving the territory? Sleeping with Rahul? Abandoning her child? We all have choices to do what we like, but unfortunately, those choices come with consequences.

I have a fascination with the unknown; I like discovering things. I think I have inherited that from my father as he loves antiques and coming across pieces that have a story behind them.

Being an island boy, I love learning about other islands, their cultures, traditions and ways of life. In 2012, I was in Rio de Janeiro, exploring the city. I noticed a lot of homeless children, some of whom had tribal markings in the form of tattoos. I wasn't sure if this was fashion or tradition, until a local back at my hostel explained to me that these children weren't from Brazil; they actually came from neighbouring islands and countries. I found this incredibly interesting, and… well, eight years later, *Escape* was published.

STORIES HEARD IN THE ESTATE

I often say it's important to be ignorant. Ignorance implies that you lack knowledge or awareness, which leaves you open minded to learn. And that is where true knowledge can be obtained.

STORIES HEARD IN THE ESTATE

LIGHT OF MY VILLAGE

The rays of sunshine soaked into the young boy's skin, pinching him slowly awake. His droopy eyelids struggled to open, the tiredness still present. As he rose from his bed, the droplets of sweat that had formed overnight ran down his face.

"Nuru!" a woman shouted, her voice harsh. Barefooted, the boy rushed from his room towards her.

"Nuru, you're going to be late for work!" The woman raised her voice as she scolded the boy. He hung his head in shame.

"I am sorry, Auntie, I was working late last night, helping the men build the school for the village."

The woman waved her cooking spoon around. "Nuru, your responsibility is here in this home. Those men are capable of completing their own jobs."

Nuru had lost both his mother and father to alcohol addiction. His four siblings had left the village in hope of finding a better life; they had not returned now for five years. The boy lived with his auntie Almasi, who had taken him into her care after the death of his parents.

"I know, Auntie, I just wanted…"

"Go, now!" she interrupted.

Nuru left his home with a feeling of disappointment. He walked through his village where the women cooked, cleaned and catered for the very young. Any men and children who were able to walk were working.

Why can Auntie Almasi not see my vision for the future? Nuru dreamt of a life where children were allowed to be children. Where they were able to play, grow and believe in the many fruitful opportunities life had to give.

Bore was a barren land, which meant people had to travel to work. Nuru met with a truck driver thirty minutes from his village every morning, riding with men and other children to find work in the nearest city, Malindi – work that usually consisted of collecting plastic waste to sell to a recycler for a small sum of money. That small sum was enough to buy essentials for his household.

Nuru rushed to the pick-up spot, only to see the truck already speeding away.

"Wait, Uncle, wait!" he shouted, the heat drying the back of his throat and reducing his voice too little more than a whimper. "Oh no, what am I going to tell Auntie?"

Nuru sat on the ground, sobbing. He couldn't go back home empty-handed; his auntie would scold him. And worse than that, what would they eat with no money for food?

As he cried and sulked, something flickered in his peripheral vision. Almost imperceptible at first, it gradually grew, becoming more and more persistent.

He raised his head, still sniffling from crying, and noticed a piercing light in the distance.

"Huh?" he murmured as he wiped his tears on to his t-shirt. "What could that be?"

The scorching heat waves hypnotised Nuru, drawing him towards the light. He hadn't noticed while he had been in his sulk, but he had been directly in the sun's heat for the past twenty minutes. Strolling towards the mirage, dragging his dusty feet across the barren land, he finally arrived at his destination.

He was standing beneath the trunk of an enormous Moringa Oleifera tree, the little oval green leaves shrouding its skeletal interior. As he looked up, the bright lights that had demanded his attention streamed through the tree's leaves. The tree looked endless as it stretched out, covering the sky.

Nuru looked around, but nothing else was in sight other than the humungous tree.

"How did you get here?' he said out loud, scratching his head in confusion. What was the source of the blinding light? Was it merely a reflection coming from the recycled metals he knew to be nearby?

No, he was mistaken.

"I just need to sit and rest for a second," Nuru said, leaning against the trunk of the tree. The branches shuffled above him, keeping him in the shade and out of the fierce heat of the day.

"Nuru, you must awake." A voice passed his earhole, whispering softly. The hungry young boy rose to his feet, stretching and yawning.

"Climb, we are waiting."

"Who said that?" Nuru turned this way and that, searching for the owner of the voice.

"Climb, child, we are waiting," it repeated. He looked up into the light, and as he did so, it brightened, enticing Nuru to follow its seductive glow.

With no idea what he was getting himself into, Nuru began climbing the tree towards the light. His bare feet gripping the ridged bark, he pulled himself up branch by branch, the light mapping the best route for him to climb, assisting him in his ascent.

Finally arriving at a thick branch sturdy enough to sit on, he noticed the light was also centred on this branch. Nuru looked further along it to where a very old lady sat. She was draped in a red robe, and glistening white beads hung from her ears. A large rounded pendant sat on her chest, every colour the world had to offer emanating from it.

The elderly lady turned her bald head and smiled at Nuru. Her smile was so big, it squeezed her eyes into a squint.

"*Jambo*," the old lady uttered through her big smile.

"*Sijambo, Mama*," Nuru replied, rubbing his eyes in disbelief. "Was it you? Did you call me here?"

Nuru was edging his body closer to the elderly lady. She continued smiling and nodded.

"How are your studies, Nuru?"

"Oh, Auntie, I have no education, I only work." Nuru bowed his head in shame, as he had in front of Auntie Almasi earlier that day. The elderly lady rubbed her hands together.

"Education is important, so I have a solution to your worries."

"You do?" Nuru's eyes widened.

"Hmm." She nodded once again. "Please, tell me the answer to this riddle: *'They moved homes and the red ones were born'.*"

Nuru frowned and his eyes began tracing the horizon as he tried to solve the puzzle.

"I think I have it," he said, raising his index finger to the sky. The elderly lady nodded, encouraging him to answer. "The fire. The Maasai often burned the old village when they moved." He grinned, showing white teeth.

"Very good, Nuru. Education is important, young one. It is essential you learn for the future of your village."

"I want to, Auntie, but I need to work to support my family. My auntie Almasi…"

"Your auntie will understand, Nuru, life is about the right balance. If you need to work, work, but do not neglect your studies. I leave you with this parting knowledge." She leaned her head close to Nuru and whispered, *"The children are the bright moon."*

The old lady stood on the branch and walked along it until she was amidst the clouds.

Nuru thought about what she had said. How might this help him convince his auntie? Deep in thought, he was climbing down the tree when another pulsing light shone out, illuminating a trail.

I wonder where this light is coming from? Nuru began climbing the tree again, lifting and pulling himself up, back towards the light. But he was becoming fatigued, affecting the way he climbed. He was slipping and misjudging his footings. *Maybe I should go back.*

A cloud hovered, coming towards him, stopping him from making a decision until it sat on his head.

"Hey, what are you doing? You're going to make me fall."

The cloud squeezed itself, twisting its core as if wringing wet laundry to remove the water. Droplets of moisture fell on to Nuru's short hair; he looked up and opened his mouth as the cloud rinsed the water from its body, quenching Nuru's thirst and recovering his energy.

"Thank you, little cloud!" Nuru shouted as it dispersed and the sky became a clear blue again.

A few more branches up, and Nuru arrived at the second light in this mysterious tree. He looked around as he sat on the branch, waiting for someone to appear.

"I am down here, Nuru," a voice yelled from beneath him. Nuru dipped his head below the branch and saw a man was hanging from it. He was wearing similar attire to the old lady, but had very long earlobes and a plethora of facial piercings. His body art sang stories of the many experiences he'd had in his fulfilled life.

"*Mambo?*" Nuru said, laughing.

"*Poa*, Nuru. How is your family?" The man began to swing on the branch.

"My auntie Almasi? Yeah, she is OK, I guess…"

"No, child, your family. How are your brothers and sisters?"

"Oh, they… um… I don't know." Nuru's shoulders became tense and he looked anywhere but at his companion.

The man climbed towards Nuru.

"Do not worry, child, birds fly in flocks. Where are they?"

"I don't know, I have lost touch with them all. They haven't come back and I have been waiting for so long. I wish I knew where they are."

"Let me help your pain. Tell me the answer to this riddle: *'Why, although your sister is so very short, is there is no fruit beyond her reach?'*"

"Hmm… because she is a monkey? No, not a monkey, an ant?" Nuru's face creased in doubt. The man hanging from the branch shook his head, biting his lips.

"I know! A bird! She is small, so small. The height of my ankle, but her wings will take her to any height she wishes."

"Yes, yes, a bird!" The man replied enthusiastically. "Family will come and go, but it is important you concentrate on your future. If they are supposed to be in your life, they will come back."

The man removed his fingertips from the branch and offered his palm to Nuru. Nuru shook his hand, in awe of his incredible strength.

"One head does not consume all knowledge." The wise man released Nuru's hand and swung into the mist of the clouds that had returned.

The boy remained seated on the branch for a while, thinking about his siblings, wondering where they were right now. He thought about what the jolly man had said to him and how one day they would return, or one day he would find them, if they were meant to be in his life.

"Ayah, my sister, she *is* very much like a little bird," Nuru said, laughing.

Nuru had lost track of time – it was starting to get late. He had better get back to reality. Sighing at the realisation that he needed to return home, he looked up one more time and noticed the light was extremely bright. It filled the clouds and poured its rays down past the branches towards him, glistening on Nuru's skin and comforting him.

"One more, then I will return home," he said to himself.

Nuru began climbing again, but he felt guilty about doing so. His auntie was relying on him. *I should really go back, this is a bad idea.* He dropped his feet downwards, but as he was doing so, the tree branch pushed his foot back upwards again.

"Hey, what are you doing?" he said to the tree. He tried placing his foot on to the lower branch, but again it pushed him back up.

"You're going to get me in trouble, my auntie will scold me," he said in frustration.

A strong and powerful voice vibrated down the tree. "You can't go down!" Nuru trembled and his eyes widened.

"Oh… I am sorry, Mr Tree, I didn't know…"

"No, child, I am up here on this branch."

"Huh? Oh yeah, I'm coming."

Nuru climbed upwards, his fingers sore, his palms sweaty and tired. His grip slipped from the branch, and as it grazed past his fingers, he tilted backwards, his body parting the clouds. Gravity wasn't going to spare him; he was on the verge of doom.

Nuru reached into nothingness, trying to cling on to something – anything – for his dear life. The light shone between his fingers and slipped on to his forearm.

It wrapped its thick, warm rays around his dark skin and clutched him. Nuru's arm jolted as his saviour began to pull and elevate him on to the final branch.

A tall man was holding Nuru. Bringing him to safety, the man placed him down to sit on the branch. The man appeared gigantic in comparison to Nuru as he walked along the branch, disappearing into the clouds and returning with a leaf-shaped bowl.

"Drink," he said, his voice deep, placing the bowl at Nuru's lips.

Nuru plunged his face into the water, the best water he had ever tasted – fresh, clean and birthed from the clouds.

"Who… who are you?" he asked, gasping for air as he brought his head up from the bowl.

"I am Maasai." The tall man stood proudly, his shield made from buffalo hide, red and black tribal patterns etched upon it.

"Wow…" Nuru stood too and began walking closer, but the Maasai warrior placed the end of his staff on his sternum.

"You must not come any further, this side is not for you."

"Oh… Thank you for saving me from falling back there. Will you ask me a riddle, Uncle?" Nuru sat down again on the branch and waited.

"How is your health, child?"

Nuru nodded, smiled. "It's fine, Uncle."

"So, tell me, why do you grieve by yourself in here?" He tapped his staff on Nuru's head.

"I do not grieve… I do not…" Nuru's eyes widened as if to hold back tears, but he couldn't.

"Why do you cry, child?"

"I miss my parents," he sobbed. "They died and left us all."

STORIES HEARD IN THE ESTATE

The Maasai warrior tore a piece of his robe and passed it to Nuru to wipe the tears from under his eyes.

"Tell me the answer to this: *'The two of us cross the wilderness without talking to each other.'*"

"I know this one, I've heard it before. We cross the wilderness and we don't talk. We are 'us' and 'us' is me. It's my shadow."

"Very good. Nuru, you must go home now, but first I want to tell you something very important. Your parents' passing doesn't mean they are dead. Death is a theory. Your parents, as I am myself, are still here. We only perish when the living have forgotten us. Love is a power greater than death."

"I would never forget my parents, Uncle," Nuru insisted.

"Yes, I know this, but do not forget your ancestors either. The following generations will remember you and your parents for all the great things you will be."

"Will I ever see you again?"

"In another realm, but for now, you can see us in everything around you." The Maasai exhaled in a big sigh. "*Teeth do not see poverty.*" Then he leaned forward, falling from the branch and evaporating into the mist of the clouds.

Nuru felt sleep creep up on him, tackling him into the drifting clouds. He slept as if he were resting for a thousand years, but in reality, it was merely an hour. As he slumped against the thick tree trunk, a gift fell into his lap.

When Nuru roused himself from his sleep, he noticed a bag full of plastic and waste had been left for him.

"Thank you!" he exclaimed up into the tree and its guiding lights. Then Nuru took his bag of fortune and ran across the barren land in excitement. He was able to exchange his bag of plastic for enough money to buy rice, bread, sugar, and even a little something for himself among the other groceries. Auntie Almasi would be happy.

That evening, after his auntie had finished cooking, she wanted to go for a stroll. This seemed a bit strange to Nuru; she had not requested to do so before.

"Where will we go, Auntie?" he asked as he walked along, holding her hand.

"You will see," she replied.

The two of them arrived outside a building. It was dark and Nuru couldn't see anything. His heart raced as he became nervous.

"Nuru, did you know? 'The children are the bright moon'," his auntie said suddenly.

"Huh?" Nuru muttered in confusion.

Lights sprang from the darkness, enveloping every corner of the building. All the local people were inside, shouting and cheering and looking at Nuru and, behind him, the other children of the village. Nuru's face broke into an enormous smile at the sight of the newly built school.

"You are the light of our village," Auntie Almasi said, returning his smile.

STORIES HEARD IN THE ESTATE

AUTHOR'S NOTES

'Light of My Village' is a story I wanted to make rich with ancestry, culture and warm-heartedness. I remember going to Kenya with my family when I was young. It is a country filled with beautiful scenery, joyous people and incredible animals.

I remember seeing a lot of street kids while we were travelling through Nairobi. Now, as an adult, I can reflect and understand how fortunate I have been to have had the opportunity for education. I don't mean to undermine people who haven't had an education because many have proven that you can still be successful without one; my train of though is that children are like sponges, soaking in knowledge, so education isn't bound to a curriculum or an institutionalised system. Education can be found in our families, in our communities, and most of all, in our culture.

When I am doing research for a story, I like to use Google Maps and zoom into streets, villages, places – anywhere that can show me the dynamics of an area, so I can capture the feel of the place before writing about it. It's the same with writing about a country's culture: I read and research it extensively before starting, even down to the names I choose for my characters. It's important to choose names that are meaningful and reflect what I want to portray.

When I came across the proverbs and riddles of Kenya, I had to pay homage. Their cultural significance is powerful. I admire the Kenyans' poetic words and pride in their way of life. The Maasai are world-renowned warriors and I couldn't write this story without acknowledging them.

The three main key states during the ascension at the Moringa Oleifera tree are the topics that Nuru has to struggle with in this story: bereavement at his parents having passed away due to their addiction; his siblings having left for future endeavours; and his entitlement to education. Although Auntie Almasi seems harsh with Nuru to begin with, sometimes our parents, guardians or carers tell us to do something we think is unfair because they know we are capable of doing this plus so much more.

The old lady on the tree states to Nuru, *"Your auntie will understand, Nuru, life is about the right balance. If you need to work, work, but do not neglect your studies…"* Life is all about balance. It's important to work hard, but it's also important to relax. If you spend all your time working and getting by, you're merely existing. To live, that takes risk. It takes leadership, but it leads to a real chance at happiness.

Live.

#WHEREARETHECHILDREN

The officers took Abuelita away once they had seen us over the wall. My Abuelita said a bad man had built the wall.

I was scared because they'd separated us, but we had to leave home because of the fighting. I knew that the man who took me away from Abuelita was important because he wore a badge that swung from his neck. His crisp uniform and clean-shaven chin meant he was either *la policía* or a soldier.

"What's your name, son?"

"Mauricio, sir." I reached out to hold his hand, but he swayed it out of the way; it made me feel unsafe.

"Here, boy, stay with the others. Someone will call you if they need you."

He opened the cage door. A metal thread weaved around the skeleton of a box where all the children had to stay. The temperature was so low, I could feel my feet freezing through the soles of my trainers. Green mattresses filled the room and children lay on them, resting under their silver blankets.

A boy with a ripped shirt approached me. "This bed is free, if you want to sleep next to me?" He directed me with his hand.

"Thank you. I'm Mauricio, what's your name?"

"I'm Gabriel, and this is the *Hieleras*."

"*Hieleras*? What do you mean, Icebox?" As I sat on my green mattress, he raised his hands, showing how they shook. Cold competed with fear, battling to take control of Gabriel's body.

The cage was crammed with children and the smell from the chemical toilets was hideous. I took my silver blanket and lay on my green mattress, thinking about Abuelita. I wanted to leave this place; now I knew why Gabriel had called it the Icebox. The temperature seemed to get colder and colder, and everyone was on edge. The *policía* were unfriendly and treated me and the other children like we were cattle; I didn't understand why. I'd only left my home because it was unsafe, but the bad man who'd built the wall took my Abuelita away and imprisoned me like a criminal. I had been told that if I joined a gang back home, it would get me into trouble and I would end up either dead or in prison. Maybe I should have joined a gang anyway, because this was torture.

Three days had passed in the Icebox and the *policía* still hadn't told us why we were here. I didn't know where my Abuelita was being kept; I just knew that I was cold and scared, like all the boys here. There was one good thing to come out of this desperate situation, though: Gabriel and I had already become good friends.

"Three more days, Mauricio," he repeatedly said to me today. "Three more days and we'll be getting out of here *mano*."

I prayed we would be out sooner. The chill frosted over my skin and pinched the surface as if the air was plucking the hairs from my body.

"Mauricio, this is Javier and Eduardo." Gabriel was speaking again. "You're in our gang now – we're *Niños Perdidos*."

"A gang? *Niños Perdidos*? What do you mean?"

"Three more days and we're breaking out of here. We need to form a gang."

Abuelita and I fled Mexico to escape the gangs, now I'm joining one to get into the United States? It didn't make much sense, but as a child in fear for my safety, what other option did I have?

I could hardly sleep. The cages were filled with children, from newborns to late teenagers. *La policía* didn't provide any soap for showers, which were limited to three minutes, and we were lucky if we were allowed to shower at all. They wouldn't give us any toiletries such as a toothbrush and toothpaste, either. My Abuelita always said it was really important to look after my teeth because I had a smile that an angel would be tempted by. I didn't feel like smiling much right now, though.

As the days passed, more and more children came in, but very few left. We were now a day away from Gabriel's grand escape, but due to the cold and the lack of cleanliness in the cage, many of the children were becoming ill, developing coughs, colds and fevers. Javier and I had a bit of a snuffle, but Eduardo was really suffering, constantly sweating and shivering at the same time.

"Gabriel, what can we do about Eduardo?" I whispered so the officers wouldn't hear.

"It's obviously not his time to leave, he will have to stay."

"No, we can't leave him," I pleaded.

"Mauricio, we're not leaving him. He's going to be taken away."

"What? What do you mean?" But as I spoke, two officers entered the cage and approached Eduardo.

"They're taking him to the flu cells. He'll be gone for a week, maybe longer."

As I lay on my green mattress that night – the night before we would attempt our escape – I could hear Javier snuffling, and I felt like my own symptoms were getting worst. I began thinking about all the other eight-year-old children in the world, wondering what they would be doing tonight. What would it be like to be American and have two parents, a secure home and a garden? What would it be like to go to school and learn things, so I could have a good job and provide for my family one day? I spent so much time wondering, I forgot to dream, and when you forget to dream, you become lost.

"You were created in duality, the place above the nine heavens."

I woke to Gabriel standing over me, Javier next to him.

"What?" I said in confusion.

"Get up, it's time. Let's get out of here."

We walked over to the corner of the cage and Gabriel gave Javier and then me a boost up so we could grab hold of the top of the fence and climb over. My heart was racing, much like it had done when Abuelita and I had run from the truck to climb the border. We reached down to pull Gabriel up, then followed his lead to the outside area where we were sometimes allowed to come and play, crawling on our forearms, trying not to make any noise.

"*Mi mano*, once we get to the outer fence, I will chuck my sweater over the sharp wire. Then we have to climb quickly. As soon as you get to the other side, run straight ahead, *entiendes*?"

"*Si*," I replied.

"*Si*," Javier agreed.

My legs felt weak and my sight was limited as the night smothered my vision. I followed Javier as he followed Gabriel's lead to the fence. Once there, Gabriel threw his sweater on to the barbed wire that was meant to keep us children inside.

We began climbing, still not making any noise, but with every reach and pull, my heart sank a little more. I might never see Abuelita again. I had to detach myself from my emotions and force myself to be brave, holding back the tears of a boy and transitioning into a man; I needed to be strong.

As we reached the top, Gabriel hopped down, followed shortly by Javier. I sat for a moment on top of the fence, looking back at the immigration detention centre. It seemed as if my life flashed before me and I was reminded of the horror of fleeing a country filled with unrest.

Just before I took the leap, I caught my finger on a sharp point of the barbed wire. Like a thorn, it pricked me. Maybe it was the last bit of hurt this world would do to me. A feeling of ecstasy, of euphoria relieved me of all my worries. There I was, on the freedom side of the fence.

I ran and ran until I felt danger's eyes leave my back and the bliss of freedom breeze through my clothes. I inhaled the sweetness of my environment and smiled.

"That's the first time I've seen you smile," Gabriel said.

"I feel good."

We continued our journey through the night. As the clouds parted, the moon became bigger. Our travels seemed timeless, into the part of the night when the moon disappears and the sky doesn't contain enough space for anything other than stars, which divide into groups, taking sides in the north and the south. We marched on. Although I was uncertain where and when, or even if we would arrive somewhere safe, I was at peace. Getting away from that prison was all that mattered.

Daylight arrived. The sun blazed fiercely, but not violently, the light giving us permission to carry on, greeting us and accompanying us on our way to our safe haven. Fascinated by the sun, I complacently entertained the idea of staying where we were, but Gabriel advised me that we still had a while before we reached our destination.

Nightfall visited us once again, but the darkness didn't bring with it fear. I wasn't sure if this was because of the peace I felt at being away from the detention centre or the company I was in.

"Javier, Mauricio, look at that," Gabriel pointed into the sky, at a star glowing bigger and brighter than any other.

"What is that star?"

"It's not a star, it's a planet. Venus."

We all stood gawking. It was beautiful, remarkable, a truly astonishing addition to the galaxy.

As we climbed to new heights, I glanced back at the route we had come, but it didn't look familiar. Nothing around me looked familiar, but why would it? I'd never been to the United States before. The stars were racing tonight, burning trails in the darkness of the sky, comets falling by the dozen, leaving shining paths for us to follow. I began to lose all concept of time, the night seeming to go on for ever.

All of a sudden, we arrived at a place that was totally green. It was the only colour present.

"Gabriel, where are we? We have been travelling for so long."

"Does this place worry you, Mauricio?" he asked.

"No, not at all, but I don't understand it. Where are we going?"

"You'll see."

We carried on our journey until we arrived at a place where blue was the only colour. I watched Gabriel's emotionless face; he seemed relaxed and certain of where we were going.

Storms raged through the sky, warning us not to go any further. Javier wanted to turn back, but Gabriel said we weren't far from our destination, and besides, he didn't belong anywhere we'd passed.

Exasperated, I sat down on the rocks of the hill we were climbing, Javier sitting next to me.

"Gabriel, where are we going?" I demanded. "You keep avoiding the question."

"You have crossed the celestial waters, the hills, the obsidian mountains and the wind. You have passed the place where banners are raised and people are pierced with arrows and their hearts devoured. The place of the dead."

STORIES HEARD IN THE ESTATE

"I don't understand, none of that makes any sense. Gabriel, who are you?"

"Mauricio, I am a *angelito.*"

Then I understood. I thought about the journey and everything that had happened. I thought about the illness Javier and I had suffered.

"I'm taking you home to the three heavens above this."

AUTHOR'S NOTES

This is a short story that was inspired by the actual #WhereAreTheChildren movement, which highlights the border control between North and South America where immigrants are being mistreated and children are being separated from their families. These children have been subjected to physical, mental and sexual abuse, as well as negligence.

I often read about unfortunate refugees searching for a safe haven in another country due to the violence and unrest in their homeland. This story was inspired by people who have to go through this horrendous system in order to pursue a normal, safe life – a life we should all be entitled to.

Mauricio represents an innocent child who has been thrown into an immigration detention centre where he experiences just how harsh this environment can be: the cold, the unhygienic facilities, the hard-hearted people in authority. During Mauricio's time in the detention centre, he makes a friend who turns out to be the Angel Gabriel from Abrahamic religious stories.

I wanted to highlight the fact that in these terrible places, many children end up getting ill due to the conditions, sometimes fatally so. It was at this point that I decided to turn the story into a journey to the afterlife. In Aztec mythology, there is a belief in thirteen heavens, with nine being for humans and the last three belonging to God's. Although, this is a story of children on their journey to the after-life and not God's. I believe that children will be able to enter any part of heaven in the after-life. When Mauricio climbs the fence to jump, he is pricked by the barbed wire. In my faith, when a good person's soul is pulled from their body by the angel of death, it's like a prick from a thorn. Something along those lines, anyway. I wanted to portray this from the point of view of an innocent child – the one last thing that could possibly hurt him before he leaves this world. He then travels through the thirteen heavens before arriving at the final destination.

Death is a hard concept for the living to digest, but death is a part of life. The idea of an afterlife differs from faith to faith, and it is not something that everyone believes in. The reality of life after death for some is no more than fiction for others. My only argument would be that some of us live long, happy lives and some live short and unjust lives. Surely, there must be a place where mercy and justice can be put in order for those who weren't given that opportunity on Earth?

WHEN THE LOTUS DISTRACTS
THE SAMURAI

STORIES HEARD IN THE ESTATE

A simple alley cat can appear to be as great as a tiger under the colourful lights of Tokyo. I have spent countless nights for the past couple of months stalking my prey, much like the feline in the garbage. When life becomes work, your life is on the line.

I am part of Chīfufamirī, an illegal underground syndicate. We are *Yakuza*. I was born into this lifestyle and raised by my *kyodai* to follow in the family tradition. I am still in the *shatei* ranking, but with time, I will rise to be *oyabun* of the Chīfufamirī.

My back is still sore from *irezumi*, the traditional process of Japanese tattooing using wooden handles and metal needles attached to silk thread. I have been granted the privilege of carrying the image of the Samurai; I am trusted with the code of the Bushido, the way of the warrior. The Samurai stands firm with his sword to hand, showing courage as he protects the koi fish on his journey. He stands loyal, knee-deep in water, a force of nature that no man can break, much like my bond to the Chīfufamirī. Finally, the Samurai stares up at the sky in hope, towards the boasting phoenix.

My target is in the apartment outside which I have parked. I have been watching carefully, but now my eyes have strayed for the very first time. The gracious stride, the elegant posture, the sparkling eyes attract my attention.

"Jundo!" As I rush from the car, she halts like a gazelle alert to the presence of a predator.

"Hansamu?" she asks. I bow my head uncharacteristically timidly.

"Yeah… it's been a long time. How is Uncle Kōfuku?"

"He is well. Hansamuchīfu, it's good to see you. I see you still have all your fingers," she jokes. I laugh, raising my head slightly, a shy child in front of this woman.

"They're all still here," I spread them out in front of her face. "I had my *irezumi* completed yesterday," I press on, wanting to carry on the conversation.

"Hmm, it was good seeing you, Hansamu. Take care of yourself," she says, walking away. I pull at her hand.

"Jundo, wait."

"What?" she snatches her hand away.

"I was wondering…" My eyes drop back to the ground. She smirks.

"Hansamuchīfu, you haven't changed."

A loud gunshot trembles through the neighbourhood, coming from my target's apartment.

"Uh… Jundo, I better go." My attention is diverted to the fourth floor of the building.

"I'll see you later, I guess?"

"Yeah, potentially with one less finger."

I run to the apartment building, smashing through each door and colliding with the communal walls until I stand in front of an apartment, its door open just a crack. The cold steel that was pressed into my waistband loosens my trousers when I remove it from its place. The temperature of the metal eases my nerves as I lead with the gun pointing into the apartment, teasing the trigger with the surface of my finger, kissing the deadly curve with the intention to press.

The apartment has been broken into. There is a trail of blood smudged across the floor, going from the kitchen into the bedroom. I creep slowly, following in the footsteps of the intruder, pushing the boundaries of fear past a once intimidated mindset. Fear is now a part of every day for me. The person of interest has been terminated, meaning I will definitely be losing some fingers tonight; I just don't know how many.

◉◇

The bedroom window is wide open, clearly an escape route for the intruder. I climb out onto the fire escape, hearing the splashing of puddles as someone runs. I jump down after them and make my way towards the market.

"*Tawagoto*." The chase begins.

Some deem an alley cat to be a peasant, but those who actually take an interest in this creature know it is an observer, an ally, and most of all, a protector. The colours of Tokyo's built-up areas, filled with neon lights, are nothing new to me. I inherited those colours. I have adapted my vision to my advantage and I embody the ink in my skin. I am by no means a saint, but for the greater good, I remove the cancer in society via an unlawful route, but a precise and efficient one. I am the watchful feline; I am the surging lights of Tokyo; I am Samurai.

Red harnesses the back of the running suspect as he turns right around the corner of the market, passing the tech store. A plunge into a deep puddle sends water splashing up onto the outside wall of a laundrette from an overflowing drain. Hacking sounds, a blade slicing through the thick necks of ducks, bounces off the soaked concrete and the runner turns his head in that distraction. Panicking for a moment as he loses sight of what is ahead, he turns down a dead end by the local mixed martial arts gym.

"Stop!"

The runner puts his hand inside his jacket pocket. Then my gun is pointing at the dead centre of his head.

"Put your weapon down or I'll shoot," I warn. Removing the gun from the inside of his jacket, he tosses it across the wet ground, sliding it towards me.

"Now show me your face." I tread carefully, stepping onto the firearm on the ground. As I squat down to secure the handgun, the runner removes the scarf covering his face.

"Who are you? Why did you kill Nobunaga?"

"Chīfufamirī, you have a lot to learn." He reaches to his back, drawing another weapon. I am too slow. Before I can register my shock, he squeezes the trigger, firing the bullet in my direction. I drop my gun in a panic, trying to dodge the bullet. I am unsuccessful. It slams into my shoulder and leaves me cradling my arm, my blood dripping to the ground.

The man runs past me and escapes.

As I lie in the hospital bed that night, I ponder over the pride and ego that led me here. I think about how I was born into the *Yakuza* and wonder what my life would be like today if I'd chosen a different path.

When I was a child, my mother would sing as she did chores around the house. I embraced those moments, especially in the early morning when the birds would sing a duet with her. Sometimes, the rain would thud, splash and gurgle along the pipes, accompanying my mother's vocals like an instrument. But the rain meant no birds. I loved harmonising my mother's voice with nature.

She didn't want me to be a part of the *Yakuza*, but she had no choice. My mother passed away when I was ten years old, dying from cancer, and my father became my only parent. Overlooking any emotional vulnerability I presented, my father treated me harshly as I grew up, claiming he was preparing me for manhood. Crying is for the weak; failing a task is for the weak; music and any dreams outside the syndicate are for the weak. And our family tradition is not weak. I thought about my mother a lot in those times when I felt vulnerable. She had allowed me to express myself in any way I wanted, show any emotion I felt, but once she passed, I had to buy into the lifestyle, the tradition.

STORIES HEARD IN THE ESTATE

Jundo and I had grown up together, but after my mother's passing, we spent less time in each other's company. My father was teaching me to be a man and I had no time for anything else. My mother always referred to Jundo as a blossoming Lotus, surrounded by so much harshness, but never breaking as her roots were strong and pure. I was distracted by the beautiful Lotus today, and as a result, tonight I will lose a finger to the *oyabun* of the Chīfufamirī. Not because I failed in my task, but because I will offer my finger as a sacrifice so I can depart from the *Yakuza* and start my life over. A life that will allow me to be the man my mother wanted me to be and, more importantly, the man I am entitled to be.

"Man is a moving being. If he does not move to what is good, he will surely move to what is not." —Issai Chozanshi

AUTHOR'S NOTES

The Lotus distracting the Samurai is a story that I feel, as a man, needs to be told. There are many layers to this story, the predominant one being that the protagonist is part of the *Yakuza*. He explains during the story there are certain expectations and how hard it is living up to those expectations.

There is often an unspoken agreement between men, especially in certain cultures, that when your father or guardian tells you to do something, you follow their orders without question. Growing up, I lived with the expectation that I would land a career in sport because my mother was a Physical Education teacher and my father was a World Powerlifting Champion and practically lived in the gym. My older brother also became a World Powerlifting Champion, so I understood what I was supposed to do.

It is against this background that Hansamu becomes distracted from his task by the appearance of Jundo. Often in life, there are people who come and go, derailing us, sometimes for the better, sometimes the worse. In this story, Jundo represents a life that Hansamu wishes he could live.

When Hansamu talks about having to be part of the *Yakuza* and gain rankings to become an *oyabun*, it emphasises a toxic kind of masculinity. After being injured, Hansamu reflects on his mother's influence, the rain and the birds and the harmonies. Here, I wanted to show passion and honesty.

It's important to teach the young about different things, and tradition is important, but not at the cost of happiness. Just because something has been done for centuries doesn't make it right for all. Real traditions are taught out of understanding and love. You can't force a person to love the sunset; you can only show them the sun setting and allow them to find the beauty for themselves.

STORIES HEARD IN THE ESTATE

A MAP TO HEAVEN

STORIES HEARD IN THE ESTATE

The sand granules grazed my skin as a gust of wind swept the golden desert, keeping me awake in the overwhelming heat of Arabia. I sat up on my straw mat and stretched my limbs like a desert cat before the hunt. Today was the day I would find the object in the sand that had been occupying my mind, enticing me to return to its resting place.

The other Bedouin said I was *majnun,* calling me crazy for leaving the caravan. I had been orphaned at a young age and the Bedouin my parents had travelled with inherited the burden of taking care of me when they passed. I don't believe they liked me much as they constantly mocked me and I was always the last in the tribe to eat.

When we had travelled from the East, I'd seen something glistening on the ground and my instinct was to go back. As usual, the others mocked me, calling my conviction *mudalil* – misleading. The thought of straying from the caravan scared me and excited me at the same time. What adventures would I stumble upon?

My father used to speak of *Khatam an-Nabiyyin – the Last Seal*. I wished to be like the Last Seal, but of course, the other Bedouin mocked me when I spoke of this, calling me strange.

At the first light of dawn, I grabbed my belongings and made way to my beloved Habib. Habib is my camel; he once belonged to my parents. He keeps me safe on my travels and always listens to me when I need a companion. I loaded all my belongings on to Habib, then just before climbing on to his back, I did something I had witnessed my father doing: I fell to my knees and prostrated myself with my forehead against the sand. I rested in this position for a while, uttering the words *"Al-Muhaymin – The Overseer"* before starting my journey.

In the midday heat, I travelled as far East as my camel would allow me to go. The scorching star dared me to lick the crinkles in my lips as it kissed me with every passing moment. My mind wandered into delusion, my body was restless and the sand was slowly sinking me further down into the Arabian abyss. With no shade and my water running low, I bowed with my hands on my knees, begging the sun to go to sleep in the clouds.

"*Ah-Raheem* – The Bestower of Mercy," I begged the One who controls the natural elements as I trod forward, dragging my feet in the sand. With the little strength I had left in my arms, I held on to Habib's reins.

The sun plucked a memory from my mind, and the words this memory contained lifted my feet.

"*Sabr, Yaseen, sabr.*" My mother's voice was telling me to be patient, giving my body hope.

The blazing star peaked, and under the sand's blanket, to my utter relief, an answering gleam caught my eye. I rushed to cradle it in my arms. Looking down at my prize, I noticed it was some sort of copper map, an astrolabe. A celestial engraving held my attention; I questioned if this was a magic or other-worldly relic. Although my instinct had been correct in leading me back to find this treasure, I wondered where the rest of the Bedouin would be now. Had I really made the right decision? My water bottle was empty, Habib was exhausted and hope was a distant memory.

Heat can trick the mind out of desperation. As I retraced my steps through the desert, a silhouette appeared in the distance, closing in on me and Habib. I was in need of this stranger's help, but I was also aware of the dangers a stranger can bring. And was the figure even real or just a hallucination?

"*Al-Mu'min* – The One Who Gives Faith and Security – I trust that whatever is to happen will only be because destiny has written for it to happen."

STORIES HEARD IN THE ESTATE

The stranger was sitting with his camel a couple of metres from me. I approached him cautiously. A small patch of grass surrounded him – grass greener than anything I had ever seen before.

"Who are you?" I was barely able to vocalise the words before darkness overtook me.

I awoke with my head in the lap of a young man. His handsome face shone like the moon, bright and clear; his beard was well-groomed and smartly presented.

"Who are you?" I asked again.

"Drink. You are dehydrated, Yaseen." He served me cold water that flooded the dryness of my throat and soothed the cracks on my lips.

"My astrolabe? Where is my map of the sky?" I asked, wiping the water from my mouth.

"Do you seek guidance for gain or knowledge?"

I sat up. "Knowledge. First, I want to know who you are."

"I cannot tell you, so please do not ask me again," he said firmly. "The real treasure in this life is the remembrance in your heart. This will lead you to Paradise."

He stood and began to walk away.

"Wait… I don't understand. Help me," I pleaded.

He turned back as if to bid me farewell, raised his index finger to the sky, and said, *"Al-Ahad."*

"What do you mean, The One?" While I was pondering his words, he disappeared into the wilderness of a sandstorm.

"Oh Habib, where will we go from here? What do we do now?" I rested my head against his. The astrolabe sat in a loose sack hanging over the camel's back. I took it out and held it in front of my face.

Maybe this is what the stranger meant; maybe the key to Paradise is this astrolabe.

The relic was held together in one piece by the *umm* – the mother – who had all her children on her back. The playful zodiac, the formal days and the misbehaving time were all in the circle of her safekeeping. Holding the *halqa* – ring – and inspecting this prize, I noticed on the back there was an *al-idada* – a ruler. I lined it up to the *kursi* – the throne that sat on top of this treasure – and using the *ankabut* – the map of the heavens – I planned my route to Paradise.

The sun took its leave for the evening and I dined with the stars. We conversed on my pilgrimage; I flirted with the diamonds in the sky as they fluttered their eyelashes, illuminating a route for me.

Following the map, content with the decision I had made on the route it would lead me, I heard something in the distance. My chest shivered, as if the sounds were pulling me towards the place where my heart had originated. The words that stroked my ears soothed my soul, which had never felt so present in my body than in this moment, reviving my aura in the chaos of life, a stream of water that flows in one direction despite the rocks and stones in its path. I was fully engaged with the peaceful words that harmonised my body, mind and soul to act as one. The energising feeling surged through me and dragged me closer to the call.

"*Allahu akbar, Allahu akbar, Allahu akbar laa ilaaha ill-Allaah, wa Allahu akbar, Allahu akbar, wa Lillaah il-hamd* – Allah is Most Great, Allah is Most Great, Allah is Most Great, there is no God but Allah, Allah is Most Great, Allah is Most Great, and to Allah be praised."

STORIES HEARD IN THE ESTATE

    People of all races, nationalities, genders and abilities circumambulated a building draped in black cloth. As I joined the crowd reciting these words, I glanced at my map one more time and noticed I'd arrived under the throne of heaven. But the map was only a guide, not a key.

AUTHOR'S NOTES

It was about a week before my wedding, and my wife-to-be and I were in the British Museum, roaming around. During that visit, we enjoyed an exhibition on the history of the Islamic world. That's when I noticed an Iranian astrolabe.

At first, I didn't understand its purpose, but the description explained that it was a map of the stars. I'd always had an idea of writing about a Bedouin, but could never really grasp the moving factor of the story. I find the desert to be a fascinating place filled with adventure, despite its miles of sand. When I was in primary school, I was intrigued by Egypt: its people, history and culture. I must have spent a good majority of my fifth year researching Egyptian hieroglyphics, mythology and language. Fortunately, my mother liked to take me and my brother away on holiday once a year, and Egypt was one of our destinations.

In the story, the protagonist Yaseen uses certain Arabic words to describe God, which translate as *The Overseer, The Bestower of Mercy* and *The One Who Gives Faith and Security.* Inadvertently, Yaseen asks this higher being for His protection, mercy and security.

After finding the astrolabe, Yaseen meets a stranger. Now I can't confirm who this person is as this is a fictional story, but if you use your imagination and link the description of the stranger with a certain figure in the Abrahamic religions who helps people in distress and teaches secrets, you may find the answer.

The end goal of the story is for Yaseen to make it to the Ka'bah in Mecca. The Ka'bah has much significance, but the aim of this story is to highlight the pilgrimage of Hajj and how this drew Yaseen into the circumambulation of the Ka'bah, reciting the praise of God.

STORIES HEARD IN THE ESTATE

Sometimes in life, we think we're lost, but we are exactly where we are supposed to be. Being curious about something unfamiliar, strange or different is exciting. It can lead to a whole new adventure, one that we may have been destined for all along. It's human nature to want to achieve success, and the majority of the time, success means something tangible. There's nothing wrong with that end goal, but we tend to overlook the real achievement in terms of the challenges and obstacles we overcome to reach it. These give us invaluable experience and help us to deal with situations and difficulties in the future.

In searching for the key, don't forget that you have a map – a map that can take you to many different doors, sometimes those that are already open to you.

KOBE

The markings on your skin; your majestic face; the ivory crowns that beautify your lips and protect your extended kiss. I'm restricted by language, but the actions of your body express emotions beyond words.

I can't gauge your fears, although I live to protect you from the greedy poachers. I can't relate.

I'm not brave.

Astonished by your presence, I remember my eyes gazing upon you when I first moved to Kerala. You were so graceful, grazing on the rich Indian plains. My intrusion didn't go unnoticed; nerves reached your legs and you became unsettled. That's when Andre came to your aid, flapping his ears. I wish I could translate his actions into vocabulary. Reaching for his tail with your trunk, you allowed him to lead you away, a protective big brother. Your fear of a stranger was mirrored by my fear of the strangers who lurked in the wild.

Yushan pulled at my arm. "Fajar, we must not spook the elephants, otherwise they will run away from their herd."

"Sorry, I… I should have been quieter."

I have dedicated my life to the animals of the world. I was appointed to Kerala after serving three years protecting the Bengal tigers in Sundarbans. I have travelled across the globe, fighting and surviving the many dangers of the wild. But it was only in Kerala I came to the realisation that Kobe could teach me more about my life than anyone or anything else could. Kobe, the one who trumpets his horn in harmony with the birds' tweets. Playing freely and carelessly like a child, he gifted me lessons like a father that would change my outlook on life.

It was under the overwhelming heat in March that I heard the distress in your call from miles away. You were lost. Part of me was glad to hear your voice, but part of me wasn't happy to hear its tone. I reached the plains where you stood moping, your head bowed to the ground. I trod carefully enough for you to know I was there, carefully enough for you to know I wasn't coming to harm you.

You sighed at my presence.

I'm not brave.

Infatuated by your grandeur, I was tempted to come closer to you, but your fear still lurked. I wanted to keep you safe; I wanted to protect you like a child; I wanted to learn the secrets of your wildness and your bravery amongst nature's kingdom. I wanted to learn from you as a student, a child, a servant. However, I couldn't let this relationship come to fruition. Once an elephant has come into contact with a human being, the herd will reject it. Much as my soul craved knowledge of your unknown animals' empire, I could only be a mere observer.

I kept my distance, hurting silently. Silence speaks so loudly in the wild; I was but an empty creature. Kobe had lost his brother. I assumed the two had been straying behind the herd, and this childlike high-spirited elephant had wandered towards the distractions of the outside of his family.. He was swinging his trunk in sorrow. I pushed the boundaries, my rubber soles edging closer.

I'll sit and watch you all night, rather than go back to camp.

The metal of my gun stained my hands, its smell industrial. Kobe was cautious of me. My eagerness to breach this wild animal's social infrastructure was going to cost either my life or his.

I stopped to think about my behaviour towards this Prince of the Jungle. It was treason. How could I care for something I was willing to destroy for my gain? I knelt on the ground and bowed my head in shame.

Maybe I'm a fool. How selfish was I to think that by protecting this being, I had an entitlement to possess him?

STORIES HEARD IN THE ESTATE

I camped at a distance from Kobe that night. Although Nature dimmed the lights so the wilderness could sleep, I was excluded from that invitation.

I awoke to the buzzing of crickets and chirping critters. The sun stroked waves of 'good morning' gestures over me, inviting me on my journey as a pilgrim. But my emotions sank with worry as I could not see Kobe.

I was exploring the plains, searching for any trace of her when I noticed a footprint in the earth. I paused for a moment, taking in this goliath piece of evidence. An elephant's footprint holds valuable information: the defined base shows youth, but the smooth edges show age. In a depth of detail, Kobe's print showed he was nineteen years of age.

I followed her trail to a lake thirty minutes away. He stood at the bank in the shallow part, inhaling the water into her trunk, exhaling it into his mouth to quench his thirst. The lake's occupants greeted her like a member of their extended family as his trunk showered water down on him.

I headed down to the far side of the lake to wash the tiredness from my eyes. Placing my gun and boots aside, I submerged my feet and wiped my face. The water blurred my version as I splashed it into my eyes, cooling the heat away.

Kobe was gone. But where?

I snapped my head to the left and right in panic. The tip of her trunk was waving at me; I laughed at her playful trickery. As he bathed in the water, I sat back on a rock, drying off.

Dismantling my gun, I cleaned it and put it back together again. Despite the fact that I was out of my depth following Kobe, I had to keep the threat of poachers stored in my head.

Wallowing in mud to protect his skin like sunblock, Kobe showed intelligence and survival skills. Thus he taught me lessons I could only learn by being here.

My radio crackled into life. "Fajar, this is Yushan. You did not come back to camp last night, where are you?"

"I'm OK. I'm with Kobe; he has strayed from his herd."

"Check-in every hour, there's reports of poachers coming from the north. What is your position right now?"

"I'm at the lake, east of the grazing plains."

"Stay there, we will get to you by late afternoon."

"I can't. Kobe is on the move."

"Faj… Fa…" The radio's frequency scrambled.

"Shit," I said to myself.

Off-course and lost, I continued my journey, guarding Kobe. By the time I'd followed him to the copse of trees, which snapped, ground and swallowed us into their midst, it was lunchtime. My radio was still playing white noise. Kobe had been grazing for hours; an elephant's digestive system is slow, taking an age to digest food.

Becoming impatient, I looked down at my compass and saw we were just off to the north. I clicked the safety button on my weapon, pressing it down with my thumb, my trigger finger shivering with anticipation as it might need to act. The cocking piece was ready for my call, the stock of the rifle cradled under my arm.

Elephants have poor eyesight, but they make up for it with their heightened sense of smell. I could neither see nor smell the poachers coming; I couldn't be the protector I was supposed to be. I wanted all the great things Kobe had to offer, but I could not do the one thing I was destined to do on our journey together.

I'm not brave.

Kobe, you smelt the gunpowder that stained the metal of their destructive instruments. You tried warning me as you stomped and shouted, but it was too late. The bullets penetrated the soft air between us. I couldn't let you stand and fight my battle, so I shouted at you to run. I really meant to say goodbye. Fate wasn't due to dethrone the Queen of the Wild today.

The poachers emerged from the bushes like stalking hyenas. I pulled the bolt back on my rifle and fired, taking a stand. Grounded, I used every piece of defence I had left in me, giving Kobe enough time to escape. Outnumbered, I knew this was the end of my watch. I jammed my radio between the rocks so Yushan would know where to find my body.

It's funny how, as I lie in my own blood, I can only recall this part of my life. My father named me *Fajar*… Bravery can cost you your life, but beauty can save your soul.

It was worth it. Long live the ivory crowns.

AUTHOR'S NOTES

I have conversations with my wife about all sorts of things. One day, we were talking about how humans have an obsession with possessing things. We love to have flowers in a vase on our dining room table, but for that to happen, the flowers must be cut from the plant and removed from their natural environment to make us happy.

Why do we do this? Why can't we enjoy the flowers where they belong and allow the next person who passes by to enjoy them, too?

I've always been an admirer of animals, and when I was younger, I had pets. In this story, Fajar is a protector of wild animals, in particular, Kobe. Unfortunately, the world is held in a state of greed where poachers and hunters kill certain animals for money, medicine or game, so I really wanted to highlight the amazing job the protectors of the animal kingdom do.

Fajar understood what it would mean if she interacted with Kobe, the repercussions that would see him ostracised by his family. She knew about his survival skills, from bathing to playing in the mud, and she knew the details of how old he was from his footprints.

There are many Fajars in the world who risk their lives to keep animals safe and untouched. There's no harm in us as humans admiring beauty, but beauty shouldn't be destroyed in order for us to possess it. We have a duty to respect and protect all life in the world, not to ruin it for our own satisfaction.

STORIES HEARD IN THE ESTATE

EXIT

STORIES HEARD IN THE ESTATE

My mother's late shift at the hospital means I can stay up late. At 9pm, I turn all the lights off in the flat and set up my den in the front room. Cushions, blankets and fairy lights have crafted a hideout fit for any explorer.

Life on the estate isn't always great, but this watchtower in which I live is a hub for people from all over the world. On the third floor, we have Mr Westcarr from Jamaica. Eighth floor, Auntie Jundo and Uncle Hansamu from Japan. Sixth floor, Nuru, the boy I walk to school with. He moved here a couple of weeks ago from Kenya.

At least two nights a week, my mother works late and I stare from our front room window over London's lights. The outside world seems so bright and distant, yet it is contained among the people of my estate. The tower block opposite televises the many dramas of life; it teaches me a lot. The stories of people and their lives unfold after 9pm. How ironic is it that my mum says that is the time for bed?

I have learnt bereavement comes in many forms, but good memories outweigh and outlive any form of sorry. Clara, who lives on the first floor, spent her youth building memories with Auntie Marianna, but after her aunt passed, she was left wondering what life would have been like if she'd had one more day with her. Although Mrs Westcarr has also passed, Mr Westcarr on the third floor is left with so many great memories and so much love that he can carry on, remembering his beloved through everyday actions.

Jesús on the fifth floor has spent his life searching for his family, his mother Josia. He has so many questions, but the questions we don't know the answers to are sometimes better for us. Abuelita on the seventh floor hasn't unpacked since she arrived on the estate. I understand she is worried about immigration so she stays ready to move rather than trying to settle and call this place home.

G

ABDUL-AHAD PATEL

On the third floor, Kapo is training hard for his next fight. He has given everything to help him win this fight so he can be reunited with his wife. On the ninth floor, I watch Yaseen dedicate his life to his belief, learning what it means to be lost, but also to find faith in unfamiliar places. On the tenth floor, I understand what it means to respect all creatures when Fajar leaves her pets in the care of her neighbours while she works abroad to protect wild animals. On the fourth floor, I see Adu find pride and identity in the history of his family's home country, Mauritius. I have learnt we should all show more empathy for our neighbours as we don't know what they may have been through.

It's just past midnight; my mother will be home soon. I pack away my den, leaving no trace that it was ever there, and pull down the blinds. It's finally time to dream of life beyond the stories of the estate.

STORIES HEARD IN THE ESTATE

THE ARTIST

Sweet Voyage
Karen Pallas

    Pallas, pronounced pal-yas. I am a British-Filipina creative, embodying the influence and inspiration from my own culture and ethnic background of the Philippines into my artwork. Using the combination of bold, bright colours with a tropical essence in my work to capture something exotic. London-based commissioned freelancer with background qualifications in Graphic and Media design, my work includes; promotional and personal illustrations, logo design, product branding and design, editorial design and publication. I aim to create artwork that celebrates memories, cultural traditions, something to warm the heart as well as the home.

Mafu
Tomekah George

    Tomekah is an illustrator based in the UK. She creates colourful illustrations which sit somewhere between a collage and a painting. Her illustrations span children's publishing, animation and advertising.

Grace,
Virtuo Mavii

I see art as any form that allows me to express a 'feeling', encouraging self-expression and creative ingenuity that builds confidence besides self-identity. In recent years, the arts have been my home of therapy. Enabling me to be more intuitive and aware of the form in which my emotions wish to be liberated, whether through Fine Art, dance, music, or writing. Ultimately, to communicate through different media and relate to an audience is where I have found my zeal has lied. Art has helped me develop the critical thinking that has enabled me to interpret the world around us in my way.

Mourn Le Morne
Rizpah Amadasun

The preference to paint a picture using words sometimes over powers the paint brush in my hand except neither exists without the other, entangled, weaving through my soul, delighted to be at work. Living in the Cotswolds provides me with the privilege of being surrounded by an abundance of trees while I explore 'otherness' beyond the other in the isolation that comes with more than a narrowly democratic location. I am an artist at the Royal College of Art by one name and a performance poet by another.

Found
Maryam Adam

Maryam is an Illustrator and Designer who creates work that is half grounded in reality but dreaming of a better future. She often creates to comment on themes that surround heritage, social politics, community building, anti-colonialism, and subversion. She likes to take quite a personal approach in her practise and build or add on to narratives to create effective, visual storytelling. She ultimately believes that creating work for the benefit of building within your communities is one of the most valuable parts of Design.

Light of my Village
Peter Ibeh

Born and raised in South London to Nigerian parents. I studied graphic design at Kingston College and London College of Communication.

My passion for art came from an early age, my mum would take me to the local library and I would spend hours emerged in the comic book section reading through manga and various superhero graphic novels trying to redraw the pictures I saw. Throughout my life drawing has been like an addiction.

#WhereAreTheChildren
Bailey Gardener-Hunt

Bailey is an illustration student from Gloucester. He mostly specialises in illustrating people as any form of expression in a person can tell a story, albeit you have to dig around to find stories and it may not be 100% accurate but that's the fun in art!

When The Lotus Distracts The Samurai
Kemal Raif

East London based Graphic Designer & Illustrator; Kemal Raif has been honing his skills in art & design for the past several years. Originally an oil painting artist, Kemal began blending his illustration skills with his love of design and tech, bringing about a perfect merging of his two passions. His evolution into vintage comic illustrations allowed him to introduce another element into his union and extend the range of his talent even further. His use of modern pop culture and comical political stances mixed with the old school feel of comic halftones allows Kemal to challenge the boundaries of modern comic art - utilising weightlessness to tell stories, which explore the depth of then and now.

A Map To Heaven
Abdul-Rashid Patel

My work has comprised of all subjects, from the inanimate to living forms using a range of medium pencil, pastel, acrylic and oil. However, my passion has always been toward figurative and portrait works in oil. For me there is nothing more captivating than a living form and the most fascinating and beautiful are human beings. I enjoy working on more than once piece at a time – moving between paintings allows time to reflect and consider adjustments and drives my motivation to continue painting. My painting touches a variety of styles including realism, impressionism and a hint of pop art.

Kobe
Hans Lundy

Hans Lundy was born in Haiti, Por Tau Prince on October 25, 1992. His family came to the United States of America in 1999 where they have lived in East Orange, NJ for the last 10 years Irvington, and East orange. He has been trained and mentored by the post-modern figurative artist Williams Coronado. Coronado exposed Hans to his ideas on using the human body as a vehicle for creative expression on an aesthetic, psychological, and philosophical format. Hans Lundy has embraced these ideas and has added the aesthetics of surrealism to create an art that is his personal view of how he sees and understands the world and art. After years of perfecting his painting style and finding his voice using the media.

ACKNOWLEDGEMENTS

All praise to the almighty, first and foremost.

This book is dedicated to my late and first born son *Muhammad Idris Abdul-Ahad.* Writing has always been an outlet and escape, to detach from the 9-5 grind and to stimulate my creative side. Because of *Idris* I have found a new purpose in writing. I often think about legacy and what I will leave behind, I think and hope that this is a project you will be proud of son. I love you and miss you dearly, there is not a day your name doesn't come out of my mouth or your face doesn't appear in my thoughts.

My beautiful and strong wife *Sarah,* I devoutly admire and love you more each day for the way you hold yourself with grace and humbleness. I learn to be a better person each day with you. My close friend *Robert Kier*, who sparked the whole idea of creating a collection. We have some wild chats about all sorts of topics, but most of all I value our friendship beyond explanation. My old college friend *Will Burden*, who helped me put together this wonderful cover and executed my vision perfectly. My brothers *Rohan Malik & Alec Horsburgh,* who helped me create the promo video and music for the book.

All of the artists who have contributed to this book. Your visualisations of my stories are impeccable *Karen Pallas, Tomekah George, Virtuo Mavii, Rizpah Amadasun, Maryam Adam, Peter Ibeh, Bailey Gardener-Hunt, Kemal Raif, Abdul-Rashid Patel & Hans Lundy.* My editor *Alison Jack* who has been with me since my third title *Escape,* your work is phenomenal.

Lastly the *London Borough of Hackney,* home to the world and all of their stories.

Abdul-Ahad Patel is a writer, poet and actor.
His work has featured in collections, online and in the media.
He has performed on stages such as BBC 1xtra,
Cheltenham Literacy Festival and The Palestinian Expo.
He has also featured in acting roles across Hollywood, Netflix and Channel 5.
'Stories Heard in The Estate' is his fourth title of work.

Abdulahadpatel.com

Printed in Great Britain
by Amazon

20991355R00069